when i was lost

jordan kurella

TREPIDATIO
PUBLISHING

ISBN: 978-1-68510-074-2 (sc)
ISBN: 978-1-68510-075-9 (ebook)
Library of Congress Catalog Number: 2022947759

First printing edition: October 21, 2022
Printed by Trepidatio Publishing in the United States of America.
Cover Design: Mikio Murakami
Edited by Sean Leonard
Proofreading and Cover/Interior Layout by Scarlett R. Algee

Trepidatio Publishing, an imprint of JournalStone Publishing
3205 Sassafras Trail
Carbondale, Illinois 62901

Trepidatio Publishing books may be ordered through booksellers or by contacting:

JournalStone | www.journalstone.com

for those who have loved
and for those who are lost

Contents

when i was lost

The Forgotten Case of Mme Augustine Calou, Witch

Evidence presented in the case of THE VILLAGE OF HARICHORT *vs* THE ESTATE OF MME AUGUSTINE CALOU. *Concerning the murder of* GERANT STÉPHANE RACHEFORT.

Presented to the court the JOURNALS OF MME AUGUSTINE CALOU

Friday, 14 November, 1834

I have seen blight come and bounties plenty, marriages fail and marriages grow into families beyond measure. As I have lived in this town many years. Many years and many moons. However, I never saw what I saw last night, and I write this with as much truth as I have always had, the truth left in my last two teeth to tell it with.

Written here, with shaky hand and the last of my sanity, is what I saw: Gerant Stéphane Rachefort is a werewolf. I saw him change under the light of the moon in my own fields; saw him tear asunder one of my sows, and saw him cry in exultation before he took off, pig bloodied, into the night.

I am an old woman, and this is true.

My eyes are not what they were. But the light of the moon was bright enough last night, and my pipe had long ago gone cold. I sat in the freeze of the winter evening in my favorite chair and witnessed the entire thing. I dared not breathe an extra breath, lest he sense me. Lest he tear me asunder too. I heard my sow's cries, heard the rest of her brood cry out for her, knowing their mother's voice.

But the stink of my farm covered my scent, and covered Gerant Rachefort's muzzle.

How did I know it was him? The particular sheen of his coat, so silver and so clean. He is the only clean man among us in this farming village. Stéphane Rachefort would be the only dainty wolf among werewolves, pausing to wipe his snout on his torn sleeve. The frilled one I recognized from the tavern earlier this week. When I saw him with his beloved sailors, the beloved sailors that I wish would go away from this lovely man. This lovely man who is too lovely for this world, this village, this life.

This lovely man who I wish were mine.

***

Friday, 14 November, 1834

Wolves are bold animals, this is truth. They've been coming closer and closer to the village in recent years. They smell our livestock, after the soil became too hardened for crops the last few decades. They smell our pigs, our cows, our goats. All of which feed the hunger of the men who sail for short periods on long boats, the meats salted and cured for their short journeys and large appetites.

Men are bold animals too.

They go after beautiful things that do not understand them as I do.

They come to my farm. "Old woman," they say. "How much for one of your pigs, whole?"

And I tell them the price. I am old, but I am fair.

"Sounds high," they say every time, and one of them laughs. One of them always laughs. "The woman down the way offered me half for one of her pigs, whole."

"No other woman is a pig farmer here," I say. "The Lilivanes have boar, but I am the only pig farmer."

"You sure, old woman? Perhaps you forgot."

They lean in, they mean business.

So I lean in too. My eyes half milky, my hand on my cane, my knuckles black with stink, my breath black with it too.

"I don't forget," I say. "I never forget."

They take the pig for my fair price, every time. But only the meat, never the whole animal. They wouldn't know what to do with him once they got him. They are young sailors, not old farmers. I doubt a single one of them knows what a pig farm is best for. They wouldn't know what to do with Stéphane Rachefort if he actually let them catch him. If he let these sailors take him away the way they want to, with the hunger in their eyes the way I see it.

All men are unfair in their own way.

Such as Stéphane Rachefort took my pig for an unfair price, and now he must pay. A werewolf, however, is a tricky creature, and must be dealt with in tricky ways. Where one lies, others are sure to lay in wait.

A lone wolf is too dangerous.

He needs his pack.

The legend of werewolves is that they create their own pack borne from loneliness. They require friends, so they fashion them, put those they admire through the same torment that they were put through.

Or perhaps not admire, perhaps despise.

I am a despised woman, as many old women are. Those of us who can survive alone for so long without a man to satiate our appetites, to aid us in what we are meant to be aided in. Should we prove to be too independent, too survivable, we, too, must be dangerous, as a werewolf is.

Gerant Stéphane Rachefort and I were made for each other.

This is why it is he I must go courting. Finally. For the first and final time.

***

Saturday, 15 November, 1834

I arrive at Rachefort's home after the winter sun has worn off all the frost and warmed my bones enough to leave the house. And I do leave it, with pastries and fresh bacon wrapped in a basket. My dog, Grimsby, is at my side, old and spine bent like me. We both hobble to the gerant's house, making our way slowly through the frozen village streets so that we may be seen.

I stand, Grimsby sits at the gerant's door for a few moments in a way to be spectated. Me pulling at the shawl around my head. Black for a widow, moth eaten for poverty, although all in the village know I am not poor; I am simply busy.

My dog scratches at his haunches. He is bored, or disturbed. He pants nervously. Sniffs the air curiously. He does not like being here. He pokes at my knee, half-moon-eyed and full of concern.

"Hush, Grimsby," I tell him.

Only then do I knock on the door.

Grimsby and I wait a longer time than we should have to for a very exhausted and hungover appearing Stéphane Rachefort to open it. His grey hair disheveled in sleep, his eyes tired, bags hanging low down his smooth cheeks. He leans heavily on the door frame, looking first at Grimsby, then at me.

"Ah," he says. "Madame Calou, to what do I owe the ple—" He stifles a belch. "Pardon me. Pleasure."

"I brought breakfast," I say, uncovering the cooling food. "I thought it a nice gesture, considering the difficult times we're in."

"Difficult times," he says.

He feigns confusion.

"Yes," I said. "With your late evenings out working in the fields in the moonlight."

He was looking at Grimsby. Grimsby, whose teeth are bared at Rachefort in such a way to give the game away. I am calm as I am among the sailors who would do me harm if I hadn't played the game as long as I had.

"Come in," Rachefort says. Whispers rather. "Leave the dog outside."

So I do, and the dog stays.

There is too much to discuss.

Rachefort sits down at the table and I lay out the pastries and bacon. He looks sick to see the bacon, but takes the pastries whole-handed and eats them hungrily. Change makes a man hungry, it does every time, no matter what the change is.

I take the bacon and break it into small strips to eat it with the two teeth I have left. We stare at each other a moment, as the sun filters in through his closed curtains to light up his meagre amount of furniture: an unmade bed, a counter full of unwashed dishes, a floor full of empty bottles. The room smells of sex and sweat. And men. So many men.

There are the questions I want to ask, but currently Rachefort's chest rises and falls in such metered time, I realize that he is at the edge of sick and I must meter my own self, lest I want to end up like my own sow. In pieces.

"Why did you come here, Madame Calou?"

Ah. The question.

"I saw you last night," I say. "In my fields. I saw you with my sow. I saw her blood covering your snout and your claws and your chest. Eventually your sleeve."

He looks down at his hands.

"And you are sure it was me?"

"No other," I say. "I recognized your frilly sleeves and such on from the tavern. The particular silver sheen of your coat matched your hair." I sigh as I chew carefully on another bacon slice. "It was you, Rachefort."

He looks up at me, his eyes narrowed, fingers curling into fists. "And what do you plan to do with this insubstantial information?"

"I propose a union of sorts."

"I will not marry you," he says.

"Oh no," I say. I do not laugh, though I want to. "You will not now, not yet."

Rachefort grits his teeth and sighs. Grimsby howls.

The game is set.

***

Saturday, 15 November, 1834

When a person has lost all sense of power, they will do anything they can to take it back. Everyone lies to themselves about themselves; even me. But when I saw the gerant in my fields, I could stop lying. His ferocity, his ability to instill fear was what I wanted, truly, without pretense. As a woman alone, I had neither, had possessed neither.

I needed, wanted, both.

The ability I had to do that now was to merely remind people that their bodies would eventually fail them, that life was a fleeting thing, and they too could end up alone and hideous, surrounded by pigs alone.

What I wanted was them to know that this was a choice I made: to be alone, to be surrounded by my pigs and my dog. That I threw everyone away because they disappointed me. That power came through my solitude and that strength came through choices.

That this last choice, this final choice I made to be alone was to turn their beautiful visions of life to nothingness and then? Run off to the woods to do it again, and again, and again.

I write this with shaking hand as I wait for Rachefort to come and fulfill our bargain. He is to arrive tonight, and I am ready for him.

***

Evidence presented in the case of THE VILLAGE OF HARICHORT vs THE ESTATE OF MME AUGUSTINE CALOU. Concerning the murder of GERANT STÉPHANE RACHEFORT.

Presented to the court the JOURNALS OF GERANT STÉPHANE RACHEFORT

Tuesday, 11 November, 1834

The beautiful sailors are in town again and I must find some way to make them leave. They challenged me to a drunken brawl last time they came carousing and I walked differently for a week. They fancy me as I fancy them and there is not a damn thing I can do about it.

This time they mean to take me out to the woods for a hunting trip. And God help me I told them I would go. I have neither skill at hunting nor the stomach for it, but I have the lust and the libido and I am a weak man.

I've cleaned my gun, which hasn't been used in a dog's age. My boots are similarly disused and horribly cracked, but I have taken a bath as I am sure they mean to do less hunting and more fucking and I do not mind if we get either or both done.

Whichever way it should go, I will come home happy.

***

Thursday, 13 November, 1834

We rushed back here the night before last as soon as we could when Piotr was smitten with me instead of sleeping. We rushed back to my home as discretely as we could, although I am sure we were seen, but made our way to the tavern as if nothing at all was the matter. The two of us carousing and carrying on as if we were simply the best of friends. Gathering drinks and women to us as per usual (and the normal amount of sidelong glances from those villagers who know better; and all the villagers know better).

The sailors are leaving tonight after one last night in my bed, and I write this anxiously at my desk while they all take a long walk together through town. I can hear them singing now, some song in a lilting language from far away. I like how they speak and how they move their tongues.

Their voices are so beautiful.

They promise they'll be back for me before I can blink. But I am an old man and cannot keep up with their vigor and ferocity much longer. Soon? Soon I will have to cease their invitations to bed and hunting trips and to the tavern. They will find it boring, but I? I will find it a relief.

I laugh at myself to think of it.

But also? I find it a comfort.

***

Friday, 14 November, 1834

I awoke today and said goodbye to the sailors at the pier, they are to leave tomorrow and must spend the day readying their boat. Vessel? I am not one for maritime language. It matters little, our time was well spent with too much drink and too many late nights.

I immediately assign myself spoonfuls of honey, and lemon squeezed in my tea. As the gerant, I cannot take too long a respite, especially after being seen with my recent company.

My head feels warm and my mouth sticky.

My usual monthly fever has come.

I will require rest later but there is much to do: a gerant's work is never done. A well must be struck deeper yet, as the summer drought made the autumn difficult, and is making the winter more so. I must be there, being who I am; it would not do for me not to be there, I am expected to give speeches and discuss duller matters. It is my function beyond approving such things as the well itself.

Embarrassingly though, my cheeks are flush, I can feel it, and there is a sweat upon my lip. Age does not do a man like me well at these times. Even in cool weather, I feel as hot as the sun.

Thankfully a healthy mustache will keep evidence of the perspiration at bay. A mustache which I have been constructing for some time now, it is quite a healthy bushel of hair and now requires some waxing to keep tame. It is a lovely specimen of a thing, which draws some men in the village closer to me. It is also a marvel of a thing that the sailors said they liked very much, very much indeed.

The well striking is in the next hour, and I require a strong tea and a stronger breakfast if I am to be upright of stature and voice in that time.

God help me today.

***

Friday, 14 November, 1834

The well striking did go well, I believe. Although the town surgeon did take me aside and offer me a tonic for my throat. He said I sounded as if I had a rough go of it the past few nights, and then winked knowingly. Perhaps he fancies me.

He is too pale about the cheeks for my tastes, I am afraid. The man has sticky palms and a sickly look about him, as if he carries all the plagues of the village upon his skin. I would not kiss him if it would cure all the monthly fevers I should catch until death. Still yet, the man cares a great deal, and he is kind. As is evidenced by the tonic.

And how he patted me on the back all the same.

"Take rest tonight," he said, and glanced up at the sky. "The moon."

"The moon."

I nodded, he nodded, and we looked off to the old shepherd woman's house, Mme Calou. Mme Calou, who would have us all dead if she had her way. The Madame would serve us to the gallows for tea and then serve us at her table at sunset if it would make her day all the more pleasant. So the saying goes around the village.

She has been alone since I came here a decade ago, running her abominable farm without more than her hound for company. She got the dog about five years ago as it wandered onto her property and, as stubborn as she was, simply refused to leave. The two are born for one another. Still yet, she is like me. Neither of us will live our life any other way but our own.

"She's a witch, I'm sure of it," Piotr said the last time he was here. "Tried to charge me an entire boar's price for a sickly piglet carcass."

"Mm," I said, toeing the line between my own people and my own guests. "She's a businesswoman."

"She's a witch and you know it."

"Whatever she is—"

"She's got to go," Piotr said, before kissing me.

Still yet, the moon, and the moon had plans for me. And I had eventual plans for Mme Calou, whether she knew them, or the village knew it (yet). We would all learn them in due time, in due time. Feral creatures such as witches and those of us who live by the monthly tides of what comes in and out of our feral natures do not do well by planning.

We do not do well by planning at all.

***

Saturday, 15 November, 1834

I woke up outside that old witch's fences. Dead pig skin beneath my fingernails, the taste of its meat on my tongue. I remember it, I remember the taste so well, having tasted Calou's pigs so, so many times.

Why do I provoke her so? Is it for the sport of it? Is it to whittle her down, bit by tiny bit? To make her leave? To make her approach me, confront me? To make her finally realize that it is she who is alone here, in this village?

That she, herself, is the one who is wrong?

We are so alike, Calou and I. We are solitary beings. Alone in our spite, in our insatiability; our stubbornness, our need to control, our need to be in control. And yet we cannot see this. We cannot know this. She came to me, as I did bait her. I heard her dog barking outside my door earlier, so I let her in, and so she entered.

"Mme Calou," I told her. "Have a seat."

She did sit. And we spoke for a long time on our plans for the village, on what we wanted it to be, on what we wanted it to become. On what we thought would be best for it, and on what we thought it could never, ever come to pass.

We drank much that late morning into mid-afternoon.

And she left, head hanging low, and I shut my door, head also hanging low. How unfortunate that the two of us, so alike in so many ways, could not solve the problems that plagued so many others but ourselves.

***

Evidence presented in the case of THE VILLAGE OF HARICHORT *vs* THE ESTATE OF MME AUGUSTINE CALOU. *Concerning the murder of* GERANT STÉPHANE RACHEFORT.

Presented to the court by the Prosecution representing THE VILLAGE OF HARICHORT, *observations and items ratified at the* VILLAGE *itself*

1) One (1) journal belonging to Mme Calou
2) One (1) journal belonging to Gerant Stéphane Rachefort
3) Two (2) wardrobes, bereft of clothing

The whereabouts of Mme Augustine Calou are currently unknown. However, the whereabouts of Gerant Stéphane Rachefort are also currently unknown. It is the opinion of the villagers that Rachefort would not have left with Mme Calou under any circumstance other than coercion. Prosecution suspects coercive witchcraft by Mme Augustine Calou. The woman remains missing, even to this day.

***

Evidence presented in the case of THE VILLAGE OF HARICHORT *vs* THE ESTATE OF MME AUGUSTINE CALOU. *Concerning the murder of* GERANT STÉPHANE RACHEFORT.

Presented to the court by the Defense representing THE ESTATE OF MME AUGUSTINE CALOU, *observations ratified at* THE VILLAGE OF HARICHORT

1) Two (2) residences. Undisturbed.
2) One (1) stock of pigs. Unharmed.

3) Set of footprints, three, heading toward the dock (3). Presumed canine.

Defense ratifies Prosecution's statement that Gerant Stéphane Rachefort is missing. The Gerant is an abnormally slight man; he would be easily spotted among either the citizenry of Harichort or in any nearby town. However, he has been seen nowhere. It is Defense's supposition that Gerant Stéphane Rachefort left with Mme Calou of his own accord, making the both of them merely victims of speculation and superstition by a village swept by curious people and curiouser events.

Calou and Rachefort have committed no crime.

They are merely equally alike, and perhaps equally in love.

The True and Otherworldly Origins of the Name "Calamity Jane"

She hunted fairies. It was how she knew this whole thing was a trap. Jane had passed through Hartville, Wyoming, about once a month for the past two years, and until today it was a town with chatter wafting out of every storefront, where the saloon reeked of sweat and booze, and with so much wagon traffic that it slowed her down. Now the storefronts were silent, the saloon was empty, and the wagon tracks were filling in with dirt.

Six months ago when Jane had sworn off this job for good, she told herself nothing would bring her back to it, but this…this she couldn't ignore. There was no way Earl would've passed this up either. He would've known, like she knew now, that there was a fairy inside, in this art gallery painted storm-sky blue with the words *"GALLERY OF DREAMS – OPEN NOW"* arching over the black curtain serving as its front door. And it *was* open. Jane could hear someone singing inside.

And whatever it was, it wasn't human.

She had eight cold-iron shells left over from when she'd given this all up, and now seemed the right time to use them. But if things started going south, she had to make sure there was one left for herself. So once there were two loaded in her shotgun, she took a step forward, but before her heel could touch down, a witch stepped through the curtain.

"Ah, Martha Jane, so glad you could come," the witch said as she approached. This had to be the fairy; she had skin too pale for frontier living and a dress and eyes the same midnight blue. There was a chill coming off her, like being near a mountain creek, and when she took Jane's cheeks in her fingers, her touch was February cold. "We've been waiting so long for this, you cannot imagine."

"Got a guess," Jane said. "'Bout six months?"

"Time is so fluid," the witch fairy said. "Come inside, we have a gift for you."

Jane grunted, her grip tightening on her shotgun. "Won't like it."

The witch only smiled, drawing Jane closer. "I can't give away the surprise. Come." She let go of Jane's face and walked to the doorway, holding the curtain open.

If Earl were here, Jane would have been more cautious. But he wasn't, so she shouldered her shotgun, set her jaw, and marched ahead through the door. There was only one way this was going to get done, and that was *her* way.

***

At least she wasn't in Faerie.

There was a dizzying quality to Faerie, where the ideas of up and down were intertwined and everything Jane said felt wrong in her mouth. Nevertheless, it was weird in here. The air felt used, like the whole world had breathed it all up before she arrived. Also, she was alone; the witch was gone.

That witch fairy had to be magical, and if she could disappear or walk through walls, she could probably do other things. One thing Jane'd learned about fairies was that they liked to show off early, which was sometimes a blessing—it let her get a taste of what she was up against. But this witch's kind of magic? Jane was too rusty, too low on materials, and down one partner to go up against a fairy this powerful. If Earl hadn't gone missing six months ago, Jane would've been in better shape.

Oh, she'd been looking for him, but he'd vanished, like a typical man.

It would have to just be her, the paintings on the walls, and the grand table set with all the food she could imagine. The smell of the food was sickly sweet, like perfume layered over filth. She knew not to touch any of it or she'd get pulled into Faerie with no way out. That was the way fairy food worked. But she was so hungry, and that whole table was mocking her. She had to look at something else.

So she turned to the walls. Each painting was a landscape peppered with people, and although Jane wasn't much for art, looking at it beat staring at all the food she couldn't eat. She found each picture nice enough, feeling like she could live in each one if she had to. Here was a painting of a forest, there a castle, then down the wall a mountain range. But all those people in the paintings, they felt off, like they'd been added later by someone else.

It wasn't until she arrived at a painting of a beach with a dancing girl and a cowboy staring out at the water with their hands raised high that she realized it. Maybe it was the shocked expressions on all the people's faces, or the way they looked like they were caught in the middle of something else, or maybe how their clothes were wrong—a dancing girl wouldn't wear her costume to the beach. These were the missing folk from Hartville, trapped inside the art, and now they were on display.

Was *that* the surprise? Not likely. Fairies never did anything without reason, made up with their own fucked-up way of thinking. It might not make any sense to one of these townsfolk, but she and Earl had started to puzzle fairy thinking out and see things the fairy way. This witch wanted something else from her, or had something for her, and Jane wasn't exactly Christmas-keen to find out what.

"Ah, Martha Jane," said a different voice coming from the back of the room. This witch fairy had a friend. "We're so glad you came. We knew you would love our invitation, so we brought a guest."

Jane whirled around, her shotgun leveled, and she found herself looking not at two fairies but into the dead eyes of her old partner, Earl. The witch and this fairy in the gallery were holding his body up by his light brown hair. They smiled at her until she lowered the barrel of her shotgun, and when she did, they dropped Earl's corpse to the floor.

"We have a proposition for you," the gallery fairy said. She stepped into the light, her hair falling over her bare shoulders, grass-green eyes losing themselves in her pale face. "One we hope you'll keep this time, as your last broken deal didn't work out so well." She nudged Earl's body with her toe. "What do you say, Martha Jane?"

Jane couldn't say anything. Her mind was frozen in shock.

All those days spent on scouting jobs, chasing old leads and older stories for a glimpse of Earl's horse or a whiff of his aftershave. She should've stopped when everything came up cold, but no, she'd only gotten bolder, more brazen in her searching. And now here he was, exactly as all her nightmares had played out.

"Good girl, Martha Jane," the witch said. "Finally willing to work with us."

"You'll be pleased with the outcome," the gallery fairy said. "We'll free your partner's soul from our realm and let the town go."

There was a pause, like they were waiting for Jane to speak. Which meant, by her reckoning, they had another boot left to drop. There was no sense in dragging this out.

"What else d'you want?" she asked.

"You must come with us," the witch said.

Earl had always been the talker, getting them out of most scrapes with his silver tongue, while Jane spent most of her time getting them into scrapes by saying nothing at all. But this wasn't a good deal, even Jane could see that. There was no way she could let them stay here either, and she couldn't let them keep Earl's soul. Yes, she'd found him finally, and the discovery was ripping so many holes in her she was finding it hard to think or keep her eyes dry. She didn't want to see him like this, or know he was suffering like he was, all because of her. It was time to change the game.

"I got a better deal," she said.

"Ah, Martha Jane wishes to counter-offer," the gallery fairy said.

"Intriguing," the witch said. "This worked in our favor the last time. That's how your man died, yes? From you trying to bargain? So please, go ahead, speak. We're eager to hear what you have to say."

"He's not my man," Jane said.

"Is that your entire bargain?" the gallery fairy asked. "Amusing."

"No, dammit." She had to be specific. "Let Earl's soul go, right now. An' *then* I'll go to Faerie, willing-like, but you're both comin' with me."

"Is that all?" the witch asked. "Aren't you forgetting something?"

"No," Jane said. "Fuck the town, I don't owe them nothing."

"This is a good deal," the gallery fairy said.

"It's better than your previous attempt," the witch said. "Your man would be proud."

"I *said*, he's *not* my man."

"But you were in love with him from the moment he paid for you," the gallery fairy said. She slid behind Jane, running her thin fingers down one of Earl's old jackets. "Your heart belonged to him, from the moment he said, 'You're a different kind of girl.'"

"Bullshit."

"But isn't it true," the witch asked, moving closer, "that he didn't love you back? You cared for him so much, and yet...he nev—"

"Are you agreein' or not?"

"Oh, Earl," the gallery fairy said in Jane's voice, "I miss you so much."

That was it.

Forfeiting contracts was her forte. Jane raised her shotgun to fire.

***

There was a door at the back side of the gallery, shut and latched with a wooden bolt on the inside. That would do. As the two fairies closed in, Jane fired at the door, aiming to hit the frame, or at least the wall around it. But her hands were shaking, and she was backing up, trying to avoid the table, there wasn't much space in here, and she missed, twice.

She'd have to reload.

"Is she shooting her little gun at us?" the witch asked.

"I think she is," the gallery fairy said.

Jane was fumbling with the second shell when the witch twitched her fingers in front of her, plunging the room into darkness. It was thick and blue as the midnight sky, and just as suffocating. Jane was suddenly in deep ocean, drowning and gasping for breath. Her hands clutched both shotgun and shell, grabbing onto anything to bring her up and out of this, help her climb up for breath.

No. This was a lie.

She couldn't let herself believe in this. They wanted her to feel she was drowning, to die gasping for air in a simple building like someone who had no idea what they were getting into. But she was Jane Canary, she knew better—it was only darkness, magic darkness, and the gallery was still the gallery, with the table in the middle and the paintings on the windowless walls. This was no night sky, this was no deep ocean. This was Wyoming.

Whatever the witch had done, that kind of power was huge, bigger than anything Jane and Earl had ever gone up against, and there were two fairies in here with that same immense magic. With Earl's soul at stake, her own soul at stake, and the few shells she had left, she was outmatched and had too much to lose. She had to get away, but there was something she had to take care of first.

So she darted right but misjudged her distance and knocked two paintings off the wall. The two fairies whispered. If they were planning, it didn't matter. Jane knew where she was going and was already feeling her way toward the rear of the building. This place wasn't that big, and since they were still on real, actual ground, it wasn't going to get any bigger. She just had to get there.

"Are you staying, little girl? The door is the other way," the gallery fairy said. She was a few paces behind.

"Giving up? Just like you did with him?" the witch said. "Riding away like a coward into the night and leaving him behind to die?" Her voice was coming from everywhere. It surrounded her, echoing off the walls, creeping out from under the table, dangling on webs from the ceiling. It stopped when Jane reached Earl's corpse.

"You cannot save him," the gallery fairy said.

"Only we can do that," the witch said.

"Come with us," they said together. "And we will put him back where he belongs."

"You don' seem innerested in keepin' your word," Jane said. "So how about three play at that game?"

"We did not agree to your deal, foolish girl," the witch said, the words rushing in angry from the walls.

"Violence is not the answer," the gallery fairy said. "Did your man teach you nothing?"

"He *wasn't my man*," Jane said, and lifted Earl's body with one arm, feeling along the back wall with her shoulder. "Not ever."

"So sad for you," the gallery fairy said. She was too close now, Jane had to move faster. "You did love him so."

She had to make sure these two never got out of this building again. Cold iron fired into the door frames should do it, then they'd be stuck in here forever. Jane had six shells left for four targets, and she had to hit exactly.

When her shoulder connected with the back door, she stopped and fired a third time. The cold-iron pellets hit the reinforced wood, digging in just enough to serve as an anchor. She only had to do it again on the other side of this door, and then both sides of the front, all the while hoping these two couldn't figure out what she was up to. So she hefted Earl higher, dragged him a few feet backward until she fired again.

"Give up, Martha Jane," the gallery fairy said. "Know when you've lost."

Jane's hands were shaking, she couldn't reload like this. Not with Earl under one arm in this darkness. She could hear the gallery fairy close behind her, so she pulled Earl in tight and pushed off the back wall, feeling along the floor to avoid the table.

"Little girl believes she can kill us with her tiny shot and simple gun," the witch said, her voice wrapping around Jane like a cocoon. "You cannot."

Their taunts mixed her fear with a fury that was welling up inside her, sending her mind racing. The mix, she knew, was poison. This recipe of emotions was what got her into scrapes she couldn't win, and had started the whole situation that ended up getting Earl killed. Anger and fury had given her black eyes, broken fingers, and a dead partner. And now, if she wasn't careful…

No, she needed to clear her head, she needed her full concentration. Her jaw was already aching from her clenched teeth, her arm seizing from Earl's weight. Her mouth had long ago gone dry from fear, now the anger was making her speed up. She had to regain control.

Damn tortoise won the race, she told herself. *Slow the fuck down, Jane.*

There was a chill approaching, coming in slow and sinister like a draft. The witch was getting closer, and Jane's shotgun was empty. She had to reload now, but her hands were wild and slick with sweat. She had no choice. She grabbed two of her four remaining shells and whispered an even older mantra: *Two in the hand is worth one good and shot, rack em in, close it up, good as got.*

It was supposed to get her to concentrate and focus, but it wasn't working. She loaded the first shell in a panic; the chill was coming on too fast, her heart was clawing at her ribcage, and her mind was playing tricks on her—she swore she'd just felt Earl move.

The second shell went in just as the witch took Jane by the throat. She was laughing, and then the other fairy was laughing. If Jane didn't know better, she'd've thought it was a pretty sound, like carousel music. But she did know better; this meant bad things were going to happen, really bad things. The witch squeezed her throat and brought Jane so close she could taste the ice coming off her breath. But the witch said nothing, and she wasn't laughing anymore.

Because Jane had just gotten an idea.

Magic wasn't all powerful. It could be outdone by the right tools, if you outsmarted it, and Jane had been paying attention. This witch really liked this thick darkness. It let her do the voice thing, disorient people, and no light could get through. Except, judging by those tiny glimpses of daylight from where her cold-iron pellets had sprayed the back wall, well, Jane had two shots to figure out if she had the right idea.

Feet firm on the ground, Jane closed the break and fired from the hip.

The witch squeezed harder, seething through clenched teeth. "What are you doing? What are you *doing*?"

More light peeked through the front wall. Jane had one shot to see if she was right. One shot to see if she was headed for death and all these heroics were for nothing. The witch tried to turn Jane's head to meet her eyes, but Jane wouldn't have it. If she was gonna die today, she'd be damned if she let these fairies get ahold of her soul that easy. No. If they wanted all of her, they were gonna have to work for it.

So she set her arm steady at her side, stiff and solid as a cottonwood tree, and threw all her fear and anger into wrenching back the second hammer. The witch drew Jane in until they were nose to nose, but Jane just grinned into the dark, putting some of her malice there. The rest she saved to throw into her trigger finger to fire the second shell.

The shot hit, sending daylight bridging across the room like signals from a hundred stars.

The witch screamed, scraping her nails down Jane's throat and then digging them into her own skin while she stood, wailing and illuminated.

The gallery fairy flipped the table, sending food flying everywhere—whole chickens knocked the paintings from the walls, pudding spread thick on the floor, and Jane crept through it all, holding Earl close.

"Stop her!" the witch said. "Stop her!"

Jane loaded her last two shells with steady hands and turned, her shotgun aimed at the right side of the door frame, but the gallery fairy was behind her, pulling her back. "You'll regret this, Martha Jane. You'll regret this as long as you live."

"I won't." Jane steadied her arm and fired.

The cold-iron pellets hit home. The gallery fairy let go, doubling over on herself as the witch writhed on the floor, becoming part of the debris and darkness. Jane walked three slow steps to the left and took her final shot.

"We will never forget this!" the two fairies called out. "We will plague you for the rest of your days. Your life will be chaos, turmoil, mayhem. You will lose everyone you love. You will never be at peace. We curse you, Martha Jane Canary!"

"I got what I wanted," Jane said, the shells spent, the curtain drawn back, and Earl against her chest. He was closer to her now than she'd ever held him in life, and his cold, heavy body was comfortable in her arms, like it was a natural extension of what she should have done six months ago. Standing like this, she knew they were free to go.

"We will follow you!" they called out. "You are curs—"

When the curtain shut behind her, their voices cut out as if she'd closed a book, ending their story, forever trapped inside by the cold-iron anchors she'd shot into the entranceways.

***

The sun was low on the horizon when Earl was finally in the ground, and Jane was tired. She knelt down at his grave with her hat in her hands. There was something she had to see to before she left.

"Hey, Lord," she said. "I'm tryin' to give you Earl Hinkman. He was a good man, better'n most. He didn't deserve what he got."

She looked up for some kind of confirmation, but she got none. There was only that wide expanse of airless blue to get lost in.

"I'm not good at this talkin' stuff, so if you could protect him like I'm askin.' Do me this favor and take good care of him, like I couldn't. Just keep him safe an' ask him to wait for me. I'll probably be joinin' him soon enough."

***

When Jane rode out, she left everything behind her. The storefronts were silent, the saloon was empty, and the wagon tracks were lost in the dirt.

As for the fairies, it was time for someone else to take up that mantle. Let them be filled with all the danger, wonder, and loss that had occupied her life for two years. Jane was done with it, for good this time. She had a curse to get to, and nobody else could live it like her.

The Warsong of Berra and Irrit

Past the tent flap, on the day of our last battle, it is still darkness. The horizon holds onto the freezing dawn while our campfires die in the slim light available, campfires untended by anyone. Our soldiers do not stir, Berra, as you walk to me, body stiff from cold, stumbling in wakefulness, when you clutch my shoulder one last time.

Your grasp is so urgent, it feels as if it is your last before death.

Your last chance to ever hold me.

I am certain my gaze says the same: one final glance, one last chance to look at you. There is nothing said between us, nothing to be said. We both know this is our last battle, our last chance at revolution. The Queen of Lies has her army waiting beyond the mountain pass, and we both know we cannot win. Our soldiers know, our page knows.

The Queen's army knows.

But it is time to complete what we must do. With a turn of the heel, I am finally released, and I watch you step away, silhouetted against the waning darkness, hemmed in by shut tents, by cold campfires. Your dark curls swaying in the harsh mountain wind, furs billowing up against your cheek. You are victory.

And I? I am shadow, staking my staff further into the frozen ground.

The morning horn sounds, played by a page, but no soldiers stir from their tents. We will not win a battle like this, the scene before us is dismal, bleak. But, Berra, this does not stop you. You are standing triumphant as a January crocus in the center of camp.

You would sing your warsong to no one if it meant victory.

For us. For no one else.

Berra the Bard, they call you. Your posture straight as the mountain falls; your swordplay dangerous. I, Ser Irrit, am hunched back with my wrought-iron staff, my face hooded, kept in shadow. The shadow hides the intensity of my eyes. My eyes that track you, Berra. They track you always.

You were the one who taught me to watch for predators.

You were the one who taught me to behave as prey.

I track you until I am beyond the frozen tents with their silent soldiers, beyond your sight. Beyond the smell of charcoal and the growing light of dawn.

Gone. But only for a moment.

I call our page over from brushing a horse at the stables. She looks up at me, at my own stooped posture, at my own once-white furs, at my own war-weary stare hooked between two round cheeks. She adjusts her grip on the horse brush. I adjust my grip on the wooden spike hidden deep within my glove. The one only I know is there, Berra.

It is a secret I carry. And will. And have.

"Bring me two horses," I tell her, the page. "I want to hear Berra's song."

"Yes, Ser Irrit. Right away."

And she goes, not questioning why I need two horses when I am only one rider. She knows I need two horses. One for me, and one to carry you home.

***

I told you how my mother smiled at me two nights ago, after you sent me to her. It was the last time she would, the last time she would believe me. The last time she would think we could right wrongs, think the veil of lies she draped me in would comfort me, and be your shroud. She stood behind then in my old room as I took down my own hair. There were no maids for me here anymore. No such comforts, no such welcome. I must do it all myself, either as her guest, or as a spy.

I had not yet decided.

"So, you plan to attack my army on the mountain pass," my mother said. "You will lose this battle, as you have lost so many others. This will be the final loss, where you will concede the war and return to me." Her grip tightened on my shoulder, bare but for the strap of my nightgown. What a delicate thing, too delicate for the woman she'd trained me to be. "You have done well, reporting to me, keeping watch of your general, Berra. Tracking them, shadowing them."

A deep breath, a memory of you in my bed so many years ago. Then the words: "What next, Mother?"

My hands steadied themselves as I took out the final pin, dark curls falling down my back. Dark curls like my mother's: feminine and beckoning, a distracting thing, she once said, for men to get lost in.

"And then you bring Berra the Bard to me. Like a good girl."

Her nails bit into my skin. They are kept long, filed to points. Painted in black and gold like her lips, like the jewelry she wears. Like the throne she sits upon.

"Will you do this? Do I have your promise?"

What could I say then? With my mother's pointed nails so close to my throat? Pointed nails which I had seen coated in blood more than once. When I had heard screaming coming from closed doors, then watched her exit, wiping her fingers with a stained cloth.

"I promise, Mother. I will bring them to you. I will bring them home."

She ran her hand over my hair then, calluses catching on the curls.

"That's my good girl."

With a golden kiss on the cheek, my mother left me to my own reflection.

***

Now, Berra, you are in the center of our mountain camp. My horse whinnies, shifting on the cold, unforgiving ground. We are listening to your warsong, a song that casts a pall over the smoldering campfires, that sets our silent soldiers stirring in their tents. My horse's voice is gruff, a warning. And your voice is strained, a warning also.

This warsong is one of revolution, one that should topple evil, should pierce a veil of lives. The words need be sharp, the song decisive, but you slur it all.

The message is diluted.

As you are, as our soldiers are, as this revolution has become. We are all tired. Tired from the Queen and her rule. From her plans and her deceptions. We have all grown tired of losing ourselves and our loved ones against her armies and her tyranny for decades upon decades. The exhaustion weighs heavy.

Hence the war, which we brought. And the victory she has bargained for.

This particular warsong is thick with grit like salt. It coats our own words in a rime of dry bitter truth. This truth: this last battle, here on the mountain, we will lose.

But none of us will be here to see it.

As we are tired of lies, we are tired of loss, of futility. We are taking the war in our own hands, as revolutions often do, with fire and thunder and smoke. This warsong is not a lie, it is a cipher. Sung by you, Berra, as deception.

I have learned my mother's ways well. Too well.

You sway as your song reaches its crescendo, and so I approach with my two horses. When your voice wavers in a trembling vibrato, your body shakes, and you, in all your armor, hit the ground.

I wake you with one touch of my shivering blue hand, never once warmed on this infernal mountain. You take to your horse, and I lead us both away. As the distance grows, your confidence grows. Our control grows, so we believe. You know, as our army knows, we are on our way home.

You and I travel down the mountain to the sea and warmer weather. We go carrying our own conversation: sonorous, languid, with hints of thunder. Carrying all this down the mountain to the beat of our horses' hooves. Thunder in a clear sky: heraldry of doom.

"Are you ready?" I ask, gripping my reins one-handed. The other is held at my side, the wooden spike concealed in my glove making it impossible to fold my fingers, to brush your hair aside, to turn properly to see your face.

"I think we all better had be, Princess of Lies, Daughter of Deception," you say.

Princess of Lies, Daughter of Deception—that much, at least, is still true. It is still true as we round the path to my mother's palace. Her, the Queen of Lies, Mother of Deception. And I, her wayward daughter, bringing you, her knight, finally home.

***

Berra, do you remember how you always sang warsongs? The first of them to my terrible violin playing. To please my mother, and to keep you out of her sight, we once walked up and down her sunlit verandas, our bare feet slapping the tile, my bow tilting wildly across the strings.

My violin screeched.

Your voice soothed.

We walked those verandas when we were young and knew nothing of war or the truth of cold. We were mismatched pieces then: you tall and lanky with limbs that had outgrown your short torso; me short and fat, spoiled by courtly life. You, Berra, were pale from all your armor, your hands calloused from sword practice, from weapon work. My skin was soft and flush with sun and joy, the joy of seeing you.

Seeing you daily.

We aged together, you and I, walking along the veranda. I became a princess; you became a soldier. We long ago gave up hope of adventure; we had work to do, the both of us. Positions to fill.

But adventure had work for us yet.

One day, when the bougainvillea flowers were long dead and the olive trees shivered, bold and exposed in the howl of the harbor winds. One day in winter, where the light faded quickly and blue. We were heavily covered: both in cloaks and furs, our hoods down for the singing and the playing. Your hand played at your hair, your cheeks glowing with a different sort of mischief, your eyes reflecting that intent.

That day when you clutched my shoulder, as you always had, it was with a different sort of smile. That day you pulled me away, away and into a closet. It shocked me, my bow falling from my violin strings, yet still held tight in my hand.

The closet door closed behind me so quickly, it shut out the light and my breath. I was not afraid, no. My heart beat against my chest in three-quarters time as I felt your hand on my face. What I felt was something else that I had no word for at the time, but I felt it in the stutter of your breath against my cheek as you said:

"Irrit," you said. "Irrit, I—"

You paused, and the space between us grew hot as burning coals.

"May I kiss you?"

My breath collapsed like a lantern flame. But desire sings louder than fear. Its voice bolder, braver, more urgent. "Oh, Berra," I said, setting my violin aside and taking your face in my hands. "Please. Please kiss me."

Our first kiss was clumsy, as first kisses are. The closet was dark and we could see nothing: hands fumbling for each other in our layers; lips missing one another's over and over. We kissed cheeks, noses, and chins. Our foreheads crashed in our own desperation, as our breath mingled, heating up the cold of the small room until our fingers, our faces, and our hearts boiled.

Oh. But oh.

Did I love it.

That closet was our only sojourn, for a while. In the cold of winter, our bodies made it overwarm. The feel of your lips on the bare of my neck, on the bare of my chest, still made me shudder alone in my bed at nights. I imagined your sword calluses on my legs, on other places. Until.

I took a hairpin from my table and closed it in my sleeping fist. I carried it in my dress sash all that day until afternoon when you, Berra, tried to take me to the closet. Instead, I set the pin in your hand. "No," I said. "Take this. Unlock the door. Come to me."

You bit your lip so hard it disappeared under your teeth. It was now spring, and the tiles had soaked up the heat of the day. The veranda was warm, and both of us were sweating. But not from the tile, not from the white walls, not from the humidity of my mother's gardens, no.

We were sweating from thinking of what was to come.

Or what we hoped to.

We were adults and no longer in children's clothing. I felt awkward in my mother's altered black and gold dresses, with hair like hers, and nails painted to be her twin. You looked costumed in a guard's uniform and sounded like coins when you walked. My posture was always being corrected by a tutor or my maid. Your back was as straight as the mountain falls, your swordplay as dangerous. I watched you from my violin and language lessons, your movements as fluid as any of the dancers at my mother's parties.

Yet you still lost half your matches.

That night, however, that night when the lock clicked and our bodies clicked and the sheets tangled around our feet. That night when I felt the slim of your waist in my hands and your skin against mine. That night I knew that this was not a costume, this was not pretending. You, Berra, were what I needed. You were what I'd been missing all this time.

"I had dreams," I said, "of you and me like this. Of you and me doing this." And I pulled you in closer, to feel your breath on my face one more time, your skin under my fingers: scars and all, muscles and all.

"Which did you like more?" you asked. "This? Or the dream?"

You simply climbed out of bed and kissed me while pulling on your night trousers. Kissed me one last time in my mother's palace. Kissed me one last time before it all went wrong.

"I think I love you?" I asked. "Is this what love is? Dreaming about you, being with you? Thinking about you always?"

"Don't be ridiculous," you said.

"But is it?"

"We're pretending, Irrit," you said. "This is just a game."

My body went cold. My heart colder. Realization struck me like winter: shivering and blue, of my mother's rules, of how she treated women like me. Women who loved people like you. I'd taken a chance on you, Berra. A great chance. All for a game.

I sat with my hand clutching the sheets tight to my chest, trying to hide the shaking of my legs. The desire inherent in the fluttering of my breath.

"Yes," I said. "A game. All pretend."

You stared at me. Shirtless and goosebumped in the center of my room.

"This doesn't mean anything," you said. "It won't last, Irrit. It can't."

I turned away, no more able to lie. "Goodnight, Berra."

I bit my lip to bleeding as you padded to the door, pausing for a moment. Your breath coming ragged. You hadn't recovered yet from our previous activity, as I also had not.

You paused and I said, "I love you, Berra."

You did not reply, but you waited.

Four tandem breaths later, you left.

The next morning, I was thrown from my bed; I was questioned. No answer slipped from my lips, only shaking of limbs, a coward's response. It was a simple enough confession, the smell of musk and tangled sheets enough of a damnation.

Your fellow guards dragged us to the throne room, spitting cruel names and bruising my tender skin, and my mother spoke with a voice that was loud, declarative, and alien to me as family. She said, "These two have committed crimes of perversity under my roof and are no longer welcome here as its tenants or as its family. They are banished in the clothing they wear with no food or coin to sustain them."

I did not look at her then.

This was better than the alternative.

I tried to stand, to confront my mother, to tell her she was wrong, that she'd always been wrong. But you clutched my shoulder and placed a finger to your lips. We remained silent.

"I have said my piece," my mother said. "Cast them out."

The guards grabbed us both again, leaving bruises on my arms, pulling at my hair, whispering at my ear. They led us too quickly through our once favorite veranda, past the open doors, and tossed us into the dirt of my mother's vineyards beyond the gates.

We knew better not to look back then.

So we did not then.

Six years later, we found ourselves on that cold mountain pass. Six years; five of those we slept in barns, in cairns, taking on the kindness of strangers in exchange for the promise of war. And we collected that war with those promises, all those people and those weapons and that hate. You are Berra the Bard, we know why. I shrank in your wake. First a princess, then a lover, then a knight in a hooded cloak.

I became your shadow.

I became a shadow.

***

So here I am, with you, where our horses stand in front of the palace once both called home, one that had always been too guarded, until today. Suspicious, it would seem really, if one didn't know.

But, Berra, you and I knew that this was the plan all along (or half of it).

We arrive on a day where the sky is clear, erupting in stars. We arrive with the approaching sound of thunder. The stories will speak of this later, how we brought our own storm.

But stories themselves are clouded things; they always speak in half-truths. Your teeth are now locked together, your entire posture scowling, but this, too, is a lie. A half-truth. You have learned well from me, the Princess of Lies, Daughter of Deception.

You say, "Home."

And I say, "Yes."

My voice dry with travel and my tongue heavy, clacking on the edge of my teeth like a gavel. *Yes* is both a sentence and a sentencing. For one of us yet.

Because at the edge of my mother's vineyards, we take a breath, and at the break of our exhale, the guards are upon us. They wrestle me too easily from my horse, and throw me to the ground. They take my staff and my pouch. But they do not take my gloves. They do not take the wooden spike I have concealed inside.

The guards push me to the ground until my mouth fills with dirt. I cannot see you, Berra, but I cannot hear you struggling. I know you are not struggling as I am. This is curious.

"On your feet, traitor," they say to me. They say to me as they pull me up by my bound hands. My robes catching under my toes, my hood blocking my eyes. Even the best plans, I thought, are violent, filthy affairs.

You, Berra, are gone.

I do not hear the familiar and comforting sound of your leathers, of your breastplate, of your weapons. I do not hear the sonorous sound of your voice. I hear nothing except the angry muttering of the guards and the whinnying of my horse as she, too, is led away. The loss makes me cold, makes me shiver. I am ice, all of me is ice, as both you and all I know is taken.

Away from me. I am alone. All alone.

"Move, traitor. Forward."

So I do.

I am tossed at my mother's feet. Once again, I see her black lacquered toes and winter-pale feet, wrapped in golden sandals. Once again, I see the edge of her black dress brush the edge of her strong ankles. Mother, like her daughter, has not been idle in wartime.

"Ser Irrit," she says. "You brought me my gift."

Her voice is sonorous, like yours. And I hear your own, Berra, coming down the hallway, strong, like my mother's. Both your voices carry weight and purpose. Both your voices seeded with a year of war.

The thunder has grown closer. Yet the sky is dark and alight with stars. Not a drop of rain on the tile roof. Not a whisper of moisture in the dry winter air. Mother watches me. The perceived witch.

"You bring a storm to my door," she says to me, then turns to the guards. "It is a trick. Shut them, bar them. Do it now."

"Mother, I—"

"Silence, you child. You wretched thing."

But there is no quiet as you are thrown at mother's feet. Your breastplate sings as it hits the floor and as you raise your body to standing. But as you stand, your voice sings also. You are singing your warsong, the same from the earlier morning, the one you sang that had you collapsing to the frozen mountain floor.

But this time your voice is strong, not strained. This time your voice fills the room with every note and word. It shakes my wretched bones to wanting; it turns my mother's head. This is the true power of the warsong: to topple evil, to pierce a veil of lies.

As the guards hold their spears to your throat, the tips shake like the strings of my long-dead violin.

"Make them stop!" my mother says to me. "Make them stop singing now, Irrit."

Her voice cannot compete with yours. She cannot sing like you, she never could. But the trick with warsong is truth, and truth has power, which is why my words hit my mother twice as hard when I tell her, "There is no trickery afoot with storms."

I say as I stand heavy with winter furs and gloves and leathers, "There is only their song—Berra's song—and the power of it. There is only their truth, our truth, and the weight of what you know bearing down on you."

The spears are at my throat now as my mother says, "You will stop them now, Irrit. Obey your mother, as you have done so well for so long. Do it, for the love of your mother, and the love of the queendom she protects."

There is no answer but the answer of our army breaking through the doors. The once far-away thunder was the sound of a hundred hundred hooves. So many soldiers and so many swords bearing down on my mother's palace, now filling it with shouting and swordplay. And yet, Berra, you continue singing, as the army continues attacking. You pull your sword, running it through the closest guard, withdrawing it, and then slashing it at the next.

But my mother, as always, only has eyes for me. Me who stands, my hood shadowing the violence in my eyes. Me in my stained furs, our gambit revealed. Now I have nothing but one spike, one truth, and a vendetta.

And now I pay attention to how my mother drums her pointed nails twice before standing and walking toward me. I watch this as I change my grip on my weapon. I know what is coming. And as I know now, plans have to change.

Our soldiers are in the hallways now, boots on tile. Metal on metal. Shouting on shouting. And, Berra, you are still singing, your voice loud above the din as you kick another guard away with your boot, sending him tumbling backward before you throw your only dagger at him.

It strikes him in his own screaming voice.

Berra the Bard: tall as the mountain falls, swordplay as dangerous. You are proving that here today. I watch you fight. I watch you fight as my mother advances through the melee, guards dancing around her black dress and gold belt and high-pinned hair.

As if she is a god. But no, she is only a Queen.

When she reaches me, she snatches me by the cheeks. Rounded like hers, glowing like hers. Spiked nails digging in deep; it is her that draws first blood.

"You lied to me, Irrit," she says.

"You lie all the time," I say. "It's in your title."

"You lied to me about too much," she says, "too much, and now it is time to die."

The fighting all around us: swords on swords on armor. Screams and shouts and scuffle. A careful waltz of leather and steel. My mother holds me tight in her grip, her eyes daring me to move, my blood running down her fingers, dripping onto the tile floor.

And she still spoke. Her words sharp, pointed, cut with vengeance.

"All those times you came to my palace, to meet with me, to report on your battles, to tell me of Berra's movements, of their plans. They were for what? So that you could do this? So that you could bring your army here?"

We look at each other as she speaks. As she continues to speak, but I know something she does not: I carry my own hate too, and it is just as vicious.

"I offered you food and shelter. I offered you solace and peace. I offered you your position back, and this is how you repay me? This is ho—"

But she does not finish.

She cannot.

Rage is a boiling thing. There are only so many moments it waits before it escapes confinement. As my mother spoke, as I bled onto her hands, that rage grew, and as it grew, my grip strengthened on my weapon. The only one I carried for so long. My mother had her nails, but she also had her words.

I would take those from her.

They were far more dangerous.

So as she begins, *This is how,* my hand darts up, heavy in its leather cloak. Heavy with fury and desire and hate. I throw off my gloves, taking the concealed wooden spike with both hands. And with my war-strengthened hands I reach up and pierce my mother's voice.

Now? My mother will shed blood for me.

It is this way that I, Ser Irrit, Princess of Lies, end the Queen's reign.

My mother staggers back, clutching at her neck, choking, bleeding. She is dying, and her guards are all dying around her. Our army, well fed on our last stores, fights their last battle at the last place my mother expected. And as her knees fold under her, and as her hands clasp once more at her throat, I cover my mouth. I cover my mouth as you, Berra, sing in exultation.

Your armor is covered in soldiers' blood, your face and hair as well. You are soaked in the spoils of battle and I am soaked in the spoils of regicide. One of us will be a hero, the other a murderer. Victory is yours, as it was meant to be, and I? I am damned.

I cover my mouth, my mother's blood pooling at my toes.

And then? I flee.

***

I run.

I collapse.

Your clasp on my shoulder is like your last before death. Like the last time you'll ever hold me. You pull me up from the dirt of my mother's vineyards to the smell of burning and ashes falling all around us. Embers light up the night like stars.

The heat between us is too hot. Too hot to stand beside you.

It is the burning coals of hell that warm you this time. You are damnation, not desire; your face covered in soot and death and the smile of the false self-righteous. We've won our war, you will say. I can picture it, as I pictured our revolution as you stood on blighted farmland, singing of it. We've won our war and it is time for a new power in newer times.

And they will choose you, Berra the Bard, whose axe is as straight as the mountain falls, the blade as dangerous. I can see this all as you place your hand on my face.

When you kiss me, your lips are hungry and your breath is harsh against my cheek. This is passion, the first I've felt from you in a while, but I do not want it. Not anymore. Not while your grip digs deep into my shoulder; not while your fingers push back my hood to play in my hair. You are sure this will end well for you. Berra the Bard, vanquisher and hero.

While I am Ser Irrit, traitor and shadow.

Quickly, too quickly, I pull away, stepping back from your reach. But you do not notice. Instead, you raise your hands to the smoke in the sky, our once-favorite vineyards burning at your back. Sweat makes tracks in the soot and blood on your face, soaking the grime into your hair and dripping it in a mass onto your leathers.

You catch your breath, looking down at me with a marred smile, and reach out for me again, your gloved hand once again at my cheek. I do not step away this time, I cannot. Fear has me struck like prey. It was you, Berra, who taught me to behave this way: like prey. I am struck further by how you speak. Your tone is one I hadn't heard since we shared secrets and long veranda walks and a dark closet that we claimed as ours. When you speak it is you calling me back to my most treasured version of you. The one that I want; the one I wish you actually were. This is a dangerous trick, and you know its effect when you say:

"We won, Irrit."

Your thumb strokes my cheekbone before you continue.

"We won the game."

Three Dandelion Stars

"What should I say?" Shai asked, the mud climbing inside her boots, seeping down between her toes.

"It's your wish," Amarine said, moving the dandelion puff closer. "I picked this for you. So please, say it. And when you do, we'll watch the seeds scatter into the swamp like stars."

And then the wish will come true was implied. Amarine was always more fantastical in the swamp, untethered from her daily duties and responsibilities in the Keep, while here Shai felt she could breathe freely before returning to town and its more practical worries. But with Amarine standing nearby, Shai's concerns were only with the muck-soaked hem of her dress, and how soon it would be until Amarine's father's guards came to fetch her.

Amarine leaned in, holding the dandelion puff to Shai's lips, smiling as always. Her eyes searched Shai's face, but she would not find the wish there before it was said aloud. Shai understood the nature of wishes, the gravity of them. She understood that you did not wish for something you could buy, or something that could be given. You wished for something you *wanted*. And what Shai wanted was something worth wishing for.

"I wish," Shai said. "I wish that we could be married."

And with that, the seeds blew away into the swamp like stars, just as Amarine had said they would, but they did not take Shai's worries with them. It was her turn to search Amarine's face, and it had changed. Her eyes were cold from shock and now distant. Her mouth trembled with hesitation, and her constant smile had vanished.

Amarine, as the lord's daughter, stood to lose everything, and she knew that. Shai knew that. And the realization made Shai wanted to send all that knowing away, down into the black depths of the swamp pools where the dandelion seeds had gone. Send them away with the wish, which had vanished into the cold winter wind. So she took that trembling mouth of Amarine's to hers, drawing it into a kiss.

They fell into familiarity. Shai's mud-soaked fingers ran through

Amarine's dark curls, pulling her hair down in soft tugs. Her cold hands warmed as they searched for skin and then dress and then skin again. Her lips kissed the hesitation away from Amarine's mouth, the shock away from her eyes, and the winter away from her cheeks. She held Amarine close, feeling her bones through her dress, and then holding them against her own soft hips.

This was what she wanted, forever and always. This was what she had wished for. She kissed Amarine until she forgot the cold, the guards, and everything. The world was only her and Amarine, together and absolute. Forever and always, happily ever after, until the sound of a horn tore them apart.

"My father..." Amarine said, holding Shai's hand.

Shai was already fixing Amarine's hair and fastening the buttons on her dress. There were no words that needed saying. Amarine's home was in the Keep, with its stone walls and standing guards, while Shai had to hurry home to the thick dirt streets of town and its smells of iron and other people's cooking. Amarine had to be found as alone as the guards had left her, to arouse no suspicion. She couldn't be as alone as the two of them had been together, the rest of the world forgotten, making wishes and bestowing kisses—that would have to wait until an impossible day.

So Shai hurried back to town, catching one last glimpse of Amarine standing sentinel in the winter swamp. Shai knew Amarine would send another letter soon, and they would be together again, one day.

But this evening as Shai hurried back toward the border fences, she could not shake the feeling of being watched.

***

It had been three days since the kiss in the swamp, and Shai had spent them practicing her reading and doing other people's mending. When her brother Yann came home filthy from his long day of blacksmith work, she washed his clothes and put out clean ones for the next day. Each night they shared the meal Shai cooked for them like every other night, and afterward Yann left for the tavern, and Shai would be alone. Each day was the same as each night, and Shai brought joy to them all with thoughts of Amarine and her pale green eyes, her long dark hair, and her thin, smooth fingers.

On the third night, Yann returned home from the tavern, full of laughter with stories of his failed conquests before he fell fast asleep in his bed. But Shai lay awake, counting the stars. This time of year there were twelve she could see through the window, huddled close together like scared children. She counted them over and over to keep them safe as the clouds drifted over them, causing the room to go dark, and she waited, until it went darker still.

Someone was crouching in the window well.

Shai sat up, ready to call out, ready to scream. But she saw as the person approached that it wasn't a person at all. As the clouds dispersed, Shai could see her swamp-weed wings, her slick sallow-green skin, her onyx black eyes. Her mother had told her stories about the swamp folk, about their tricks and promises, and how Shai must always act around them—polite and careful. She could hear her mother's voice, "Remember, with the swamp fairies, you must only expect what you do not expect."

"I have come to grant your wish," the swamp fairy said, her head moving snake-like on her shoulders. "But I require something in return."

Shai wanted nothing more than this. It was the only thing she had ever wanted since Amarine had first kissed her five happy years ago. There would be consequences, not only the swamp fairy's, but within the town. But she and Amarine would be happy, Shai would see to that.

"What are the conditions?" Shai asked.

"The conditions are mine to consider," the swamp fairy said. "The consequences yours. Do you accept?"

"What will you need?"

"Only three stars," she said. "Three dandelion seeds fell into my pool, so I will take three stars from you."

"I don't understand." Shai looked at her brother's bed; he was still sleeping soundly.

"Shooting stars," the swamp fairy said. "Your first three falling stars of spring. From the moment they fall, the night belongs to me."

The fairy held up three webbed fingers, and Shai turned to her brother, his chest still rising and falling in sleep. He wouldn't approve. Ever since their mother had run away, and their father died along with nineteen other men when trying to bring her to justice, Yann hovered over Shai, curious about everything she did. So she shared nothing of her life. Nothing about how she missed their mother, nothing about Amarine, nothing about her walks in the woods. In recent years, Yann had stopped asking questions, and Shai enjoyed her freedom. She lived her life of secrets as he lived his life without them.

But she couldn't stay here with him. He would have her marry someone to make them rich; someone to elevate their standing. Amarine would be taken from her, only seen at town functions where Shai played the dutiful wife role to a man she didn't care for, while the life she did care for stood within reach, but like most things too beautiful for this world, she would not be allowed to touch it.

No, she was done with Yann and the life he wanted so much for both of them. Shai was her mother's daughter. She was strong like her, proud like her, and would fight for her life like her. It was time for her to become her own woman.

"I accept these terms," Shai said. "Please grant my wish. It would do me honor."

"It is yours," the swamp fairy said, touching the tip of her finger to Shai's forehead. "Now sleep."

And she did.

***

Shai remembered the ceremony as a dreamlike small, intimate affair. Just her and Amarine, with the priest from the village rushing through his words in a whisper that competed with the sounds of the dying winter wind. The story Amarine told of the ceremony had hundreds of monsters in attendance, the swamp lit by will-o-the-wisps, and her ring slipped on with cold fingers she could still feel. They claimed the abandoned cottage in the woods beyond the swamp as their new home. The floorboards were full of holes, the roof leaked, and it was rumored to be haunted, but Shai couldn't be happier. It felt welcoming to her, more like home than home had felt in years.

The morning after they were married, flowers had pushed themselves out of the mud to show off to whatever sunshine they could find. Spring was closing in, chasing winter out with its bright color.

As the weeks passed and the world started to smell new again, Shai built rabbit snares as Amarine sat at the window, gazing out at the mists rising off the swamp, lifting whatever burden she carried from her shoulders with heavy sighs. With every day Shai spent setting her traps and gathering food like her mother had taught her, Amarine's mood grew darker.

"It's too cold," she complained in the mornings.

"I am so hungry," she would say after dinner was done.

"The night is angry," she said every night as the wind ripped through the rotten wood planks.

Each of these times, Shai wrapped Amarine in her arms to soothe her. She knew Amarine was too delicate, used to the Keep with its heavy walls where nothing was ever damp or cold. And now she was out here with Shai in a cottage so rotten it sometimes smelled of death and so precarious, children told wild stories about it.

So while she stroked Amarine's dark hair, she told her stories about how the two of them befriended the ghosts, and the ghosts made the house warm for them, and into a home. And Shai did this every night, until Amarine's grip eventually grew soft, and then slack, and then her breathing became heavy with sleep.

But still as the meadow came to life, Shai caught Amarine looking out the window, her cheek in her hand, staring at nothing. It was where Shai would find her when she came in with the day's food, when she was cooking, doing the mending, tidying up. Amarine was a sad princess that would need rescuing in the fairy stories, but this was a different story entirely. Gone was the clever light from Amarine's eyes, where she had always been thinking, imagining, and telling stories. Gone was the warmth from her cheeks and her hands, as the cottage had stolen it from her. Gone was the mirth from her voice and gestures. Melancholy had overtaken Amarine, and it threatened to overtake them both, if Shai could not beat it back.

Shai had to rescue Amarine, as she had to rescue herself.

She imagined herself on a white horse, decked in armor. She imagined herself riding up to the cottage, sword in her hand, and calling the melancholy out to battle. The battle was fierce and furious. Some days she won, and she could help Amarine. Some days the melancholy beat her back, and Shai was then beaten. But she knew she had to be the knight in this story and every story, like all the ones Amarine told. And she was. As whenever she took Amarine's hand, she smiled sweetly. When they kissed, the world exploded with wildflowers. Yet in all the times between, there was Amarine, with her heavy-lidded eyes and deep sighs, filling Shai's heart with despair.

Perhaps she had made the wrong wish, or asked for the wrong thing. This was not what she had wanted, not at all.

***

Shai's mother had taught her well, but some things could not be gathered from the land. They needed simple provisions: bowls, spoons, cloth for clothes and blankets. Fearing retaliation from Yann or any of the Keep guards, Shai traveled to town only at dusk, when the shops were closing down, thinking the shopkeepers would be distracted. She disguised herself in Amarine's cloak, which had a hood to hide her face, and a pair of her gloves. Neither of them fit. The cloak was too long, and the gloves too tight. Still, they did the job, as after three trips, Shai had still not been discovered.

This time Amarine wanted a teapot, and Shai would do anything to make her wife smile, so she made for town as darkness fell. But the sound of screams and clashing swords stopped her before she reached the border fences, and with it, fear. Amarine's father would have prevented anyone from attacking the town, so if this was happening, what had happened at the Keep?

She rushed forward, climbing the fences in her skirts and cloak, and darted out into the road. Heavy mists covered everything, obscuring the cries of pain and sounds of battle in a kind of dreamlike helplessness. Shai needed to know. In times of trouble, people gathered in the tavern for sanctuary; now would be no different. It would be dangerous, but she had no choice.

She took two steps forward when a figure burst out from the mists in front of her. Their body swayed, snake-like, in front of her, and their dark, mud-cloaked armor faded into the waning light. Shai remained still. She did not speak, not wanting to provoke the stranger, whose sword still dripped with the blood of their last kill. Before she could look away, the stranger's eyes met hers. They were onyx black, and the cheeks behind the dirt and bloodstains were a slick sallow green. Shai stepped back, raising her arms to protect her face, but the stranger only smiled with a mouth full of needle-thin teeth. And then as quickly as they arrived, they were gone.

Shai fell to her knees. She was alive, and suddenly aware of the silence from town.

***

"Lord's dead," the town's tailor said. He was taking up two barstools in familiar posture with the bartender. "Slain precise like, by those strange swordsmen."

"Precise?" the bartender said, his voice and eyes level to keep the peace. "How d'you know?"

"Son's a guardsman," the tailor said. "He survived. Said they skipped him by. Them bastards were only attacking specific people on a path, ignoring everyone else. Let everyone else live, including the lord's youngest son."

"*That* sickly little thing?" the bartender said. "They kill his alchemist?"

"Aye," the tailor said. "Shame. Damn shame."

Shai leaned forward, straining to hear the conversation from her table at the rear of the room. The tavern wasn't crowded, but she needed to be in shadow, so here she sat. But as patrons filed in, the conversation became more and more difficult to make out.

"…boy won't survive the year, don't know what we'll do."

"There's always Amarine," the bartender said. "She'll do what's good for us."

"Can't do nothing as long as that witch has her," the tailor said. He leaned in close, but increased his volume; he wanted to be heard. "That girl was just like her mother, like I always said. Her father couldn't control her, her brother neither. Now look what happened."

"You blaming this attack on Shai?" The bartender's voice was just as loud. "She's not that kind of girl."

"Just cause you're sweet on that thing…"

A darker shadow jumped over Shai's table, breaking her concentration. She fell back, ready to defend herself with the dull skinning knife in her pocket, but the shadow remained, looming, waiting.

"Drink, stranger?" the shadow asked. It was only the barmaid, looking unfriendly.

"Wine," Shai said, as the conversation at the bar continued.

"Mug or a glass?" The barmaid was smiling at her, all teeth, no mirth. Did she recognize her?

"Mug," she said, tossing payment on the table.

"Good." The barmaid's smile remained loveless as she made her way to other patrons.

The conversation between the tailor and bartender was drowned out by other story pieces. "They came in from nowhere." "Snuck in quiet as ghosts." "Blades cut like magic." The talking was unlike the conversation at the bar; it was afraid and urgent, and in want of action.

Before her drink was done, she was joined at her table by a girl her age and her twin young brothers. Shai recognized the girl as the miller's daughter, Baelin. She knew Baelin from town meetings, festivals, and solstice celebrations at the Keep. They'd had conversations, played games, and their mothers had been friendly once, before everything had gone wrong. Baelin still blamed Shai for it.

Baelin could recognize Shai, and her disguise would be forfeit. The punishment for witchcraft was death. All she had to do was look up, and Shai would lose everything. It was too dangerous to stay. So she stood up from her seat just as the tavern erupted into applause.

A man had stepped onto a table in front of her. His back was to her as he took a bow, but there was something familiar about him. The dark cast to his blond hair. The black grime around his fingernails that would never scrub away, and how his grey shirt was still stubbornly white due to nightly washings. Yann raised his arms, and the cheers fell silent. Shai could not leave now.

"Our lord is dead," Yann said. "All his eligible heirs with him."

"Your sister stole off with one," a woman called out. "She learned too much from your mother."

"That she did," Yann said. "And I'm here to end that. We're going to take back Amarine by killing that witch."

The crowd fell into whispers. The murmur moved across them while Yann stood, firm and solid on the table, resolute. It was some time before someone spoke up. "You would kill your own sister?"

"That *thing* is no longer a sister of mine."

"The king should know about this," the bartender said.

"So he can appoint that sickly thing in the Keep?" Yann said. "No, we need action now. Once we rescue Amarine, I will marry her, and I will become lord." The murmurs rose up again, this time with greater volume.

It was Baelin who started the applause first, slowly to get others to follow. And follow they did, with cheers, whistles, and then by converging on Yann. The patrons at the tables drank happily, looking around, pulling friends and lovers close. The evening's previous slaughter was misdirected onto vengeance. Blood for blood, they would take what they believed was theirs.

She turned to go, she had to go. With the distraction surrounding Yann, now was the perfect time to leave. Her heart was lunging against her chest, urging her out into the night, where she could be free.

"It's not safe to leave yet, stranger," Baelin said. "Those were fairy soldiers. I've read the stories. Someone must have drawn their anger."

"Might be the witch," one of the brothers said. "Maybe she wants to be lord."

"My home is close," Shai said. Her voice was hoarse from the dryness of her throat.

"Is it?" Baelin asked. "Then why do you hide your face if you are so familiar here?" Shai could feel Baelin's judgmental stare. Suspicion had been roused, and Yann was too close to this table, making the rounds. She couldn't let him see her face, hear her voice.

Without a word to Baelin, Shai sifted through the drunks to the tavern door. On the street, the corpses of the fallen were covered in bloodied sheets, ready for the wagon to collect them in the morning. She walked quickly, exiting through the town gates as a visitor or local farmer would. She took care to see she wasn't followed.

In the clarity of fear, she noticed the apple blossoms in full bloom, and the crops in the fields peeking up above the black dirt. Spring had come, and with it so must have the fairy's first falling star. Shai walked faster. Was the fairy soldiers' attack because of her? Was Yann's betrayal because of her? Was Amarine's father dead because of her? The fairy wanted this for a reason only it knew; like her mother had always said, "There is no happily ever after, there is always a price."

And in all this, Shai had forgotten about Amarine, home alone in the rotting cottage at the edge of the swamp. Against all warnings not to, Shai cut through a farmer's yard, climbed the border fence, and ran through the woods, through the swamp, and arrived at home breathless, her mind racing with worry, only to hear singing coming from inside.

"I am so glad you're here, my love," Amarine said, resting her hand on Shai's cheek. "You were gone for so long, I had started to worry."

Her cloak was soaked with swamp muck, and her gloves slick with sweat, but Amarine, usually fussy about these things, hung up the cloak and gloves without comment and helped Shai to her seat, which was set with flowers and candles, better than Shai had ever done. She wore a contented smile on her face, one that Shai had never seen before. She had always seen smiles borne from joy or happiness, the ones Amarine wore in the swamps, but this was different. It was so comfortable there.

"I thought you may be angry at me, so I went and checked your traps and made us dinner," Amarine said.

"How did you learn to make rabbit stew?" Shai asked when their bowls were full.

"I've been paying attention," Amarine said. "Father always said I was a quick study."

Shai said nothing. With Amarine's mention of her father, her appetite was gone.

"Why were you gone so long?" Amarine asked.

"The town was attacked," Shai said. "I took shelter in the tavern with the others. Many were killed. The streets are littered with corpses."

"Oh?" Amarine's eyes were calm, collected. She was unmoved.

"Amarine," Shai said, touching her wife's hand. "Your father and brothers are dead."

Amarine only nodded. "We are alive, Shai. You and me. That is all that matters." She did not blink. "Eat, don't let it get cold."

"But…"

"My father did not want us to be happy, I want us to be happy," Amarine said, meeting Shai's eyes. "Are you happy?"

"I am," Shai said. "Are you?"

"I am," Amarine said. "My father's hold over me is over. Let us celebrate that. Let us be happy together."

It was sudden behavior. Strange, but perfect. Shai was relieved and overwhelmed with Amarine's change of heart. She refused to believe that it could be fairy magic. It was true love. The love her wife proclaimed for her on their wedding day, and the love Shai had which grew for her wife with each passing breath. She knew this was true, she had proof. Each time they kissed, it mended Amarine's tears; each time they clasped hands, it made Amarine smile. Shai had sometimes been able to dispel Amarine's melancholy with her adoration before, and now it was truly gone; what could be more magical than that?

It was all she ever wanted, all they both ever wanted. And now they had it.

She knew Amarine loved her. These past few months must have just been homesickness. Now Amarine knew her home was with her, in the cottage, because they were here together, forever. The stories of the ghosts had warmed her heart, the hand holding, the gentle caresses, all of it had brought Amarine to her. Shai sealed shut her own doubts, watching only the light in Amarine's eyes become bright with hope.

As they lay in bed that night, Amarine's kisses banished the fairy riders from Shai's mind. They banished thoughts of Yann, the swamp folk, and falling stars. The night was only Amarine.

Shai was finally happy and content.

***

The following morning the draft that passed through the walls whispered with the scent of spring, and the rain falling through the roof was fresh and warm. Shai spent the morning with Amarine collecting food and herbs, teaching her which plants in the forest were edible, as her own mother had taught her years ago. In the afternoon, they cooked together, told stories together, and held hands on their walk through the swamp. Shai listened to every word as Amarine's voice swelled with joy as she talked about how they would keep warm by the fire as old women in the cottage, ignoring the town, ignoring everyone, because they only had to answer to each other alone.

Shai couldn't tell Amarine about Yann's plan. She couldn't tell her about the town's opinion of her, or their want to steal Amarine away. She wanted to stay in the woods forever, to live off the land, to go without the town's resources, but she couldn't. Their skinning knife had broken.

That evening, in town at the tannery, Shai heard a familiar voice. Baelin was nearby, talking to an older woman Shai's mother would have known.

"Yann will make a good lord," the older woman said.

"You think Amarine will marry him?" Baelin asked. "She's always been a strange one."

"She will have no choice," the older woman said. "It's for the good of the town. She'll do it, I'm certain."

"I suppose," Baelin said.

"You should have your husband join in the hunt," the older woman said. "Yann is having trouble gathering the men he needs."

"After what happened to his father, I am not surprised. This town needs their men, and they are worried. Dispatching witches has a sour history here." Baelin shifted her weight, turning to face Shai, who pulled the hood tight around her face. But there was something about Baelin's eyes that held Shai in place, even though she wanted to run.

"Aye," the old woman said. "Damn shame his sister turned out the way she did."

When Shai was able to leave, she went out through the gates, her fear of Baelin and Yann boiling in her head. She did not check if she was being followed, not from the tannery, not from the town gates, not from the dirt path by the farmers' fields. There was no other sound but her own footsteps, her own heavy breathing, and a fox screaming in the fog.

But yet, she was unsurprised when someone grabbed her arm as she turned to leave the road.

"Stranger." It was Baelin's voice. "Are you spying on me?"

Shai kept her head bowed low. "It was you who sat at *my* table that night, not me at yours."

"But now I find you listening in on *my* conversations, *my* plans," Baelin said.

Only then did Shai tear her arm away. "No. You do that to yourself. Now let me be."

"I know who you are, Shai Ironsmith, and I know where you are hiding. Soon Yann will too, and so will his men, and their hounds."

"How do you know where we are hiding?"

But Baelin only smiled. "I will spare Amarine, for your sake," she said. "But you will not be so lucky."

And she shoved Shai away like garbage, sending her stumbling through the grass before she could catch her footing, all the while Baelin's stare fixed her, was tracking her. That feeling washed away all the happiness Shai had before arriving in town. It bored a hole through the day, sending all the good memories tumbling out.

But there was still the swamp fairy's promise. Another star could fall and change Shai's life forever, both Shai's and Amarine's. Baelin could turn into a tree in the middle of the road; Yann could drown in his soup;

the town could welcome them with open arms; somehow, someway, it *could still* be the happiness she had wished for.

The feeling of Baelin's stare was gone; Shai was too deep in the swamp now. She pounded off her worries through the swamp muck—there were too many things she wanted, that she would die for: Amarine's smile as the first and last thing of every day, the taste of her breath on her tongue, the feel of her tiny fingers against her own skin. Shai's breath became quicker the closer she got to home, and with each inhale, she made herself believe she was happy.

Amarine wanted to plant a garden, and she was wild with her plans. Shai watched her wife's lips as she went on and on about which vegetables would winter well. Amarine had chipped a tooth yesterday while chopping wood, and it gave her beauty a feral quality. Now she looked dangerous and wild. Shai liked catching glimpses of it while she talked. Shai had too much she couldn't say, so she left Amarine to hold her in her sway.

In bed that night, Amarine ran her hands over Shai's body, but Shai pushed them away. "Not tonight," she said. "I'm filthy from traveling."

"I don't care," Amarine said. "I'm filthy too."

"Please," Shai said. "In the morning."

Reluctantly, Amarine kissed Shai on the temple. "Get some rest then. You'll need it for the morning."

The night was black when the knock came at the door. It was loud, authoritative, but small. Amarine woke, staring, her green eyes looking like swamp pools in the dark. Shai stood, grabbing the skinning knife. She'd have preferred the axe, carelessly left outside, but the knife would have to do. Baelin's warning rang fresh in her ears.

"Who's there?" Amarine asked, her hands clutched at her chest. "Announce yourself."

A third knock came as a question. Shai opened the door with caution, and found only a young boy—not more than five—standing outside.

"Are you lost?" Shai asked.

No answer.

"Where's your mother?" Shai had always been suspicious of strangers.

The boy shook his head, pointing out into the dark toward the swamp.

Amarine had joined them at the door. "Oh, let the poor thing in, he'll catch cold out there in the damp."

Shai started a fire while Amarine bundled the boy up in a blanket. She held him on her lap, rocking him back and forth until he stopped shivering. The stew was warming and the fire was throwing shadows across the room as Shai stood alone and growing lonely. Something disturbed her about the boy. He kept his mouth closed when he smiled, and his hair was too thin for how tall he was. It was off-putting; he looked wrong, he acted wrong, and she felt wrong around him, but she kept herself to herself. To this boy she would be only a woman alone with her friend Amarine, not a witch at all.

He lost himself in the blankets and wrapped his arms around Amarine while she told him stories. All Shai's favorites about gallant knights and their battles to save fair maidens. She told other stories as well, about men who were in love with princesses, but how those princesses were in love with other men—ones who could turn into dragons. She told stories of girls who could do no wrong, and the magical punishments that befell them. The boy never once looked at Shai; his dark eyes were locked on Amarine as her stories moved to those about the swamp folk.

"Their gifts are grand but always given with a price," she said. "So always be kind to them, and never ever be rude."

The boy ate his stew slowly, allowing all of Amarine's stories to unfold, more and more of them that Shai had never heard, each more unbelievable than the last. Between tiny bites, he laid his head on Amarine's chest and asked for details between details, and Amarine gave them. The two of them became more beautiful than any tapestry Shai had ever seen: Amarine wove out the beauty of the swamp folk kingdom, and the nuances of dragon magic; the shine of the sun on a knight's sword, and the spray of blood from a fallen foe; and how to tell whether a fairy was being polite or cunning.

As the stories wove tighter, they cocooned Amarine and the boy up in their fantastical kingdoms and heroes and villains, and Shai was pushed away. She was alone in the shadows cast by the firelight and the smell of stew and damp and the feeling in the cottage that she was never alone. Amarine and the boy became the center of the worlds they were creating around themselves, and when Shai had had enough and felt like she couldn't reach either of them anymore and they were worlds apart and she would die of heartbreak, she heard birdsong.

Dawn had broken.

Light crept through the cottage, as if afraid to interrupt, and when it reached Amarine's toes, she caught her breath as if waking up from a nightmare. The boy unwound himself from her arms and the blanket and stood. In the light, Shai could see his slick sallow-green skin, his webbed fingers, his onyx black eyes. She felt hollow when she glanced at Amarine, whose own eyes only held affection for the boy.

"I feel better now," he said.

"You never told us your name," Amarine said.

"Pic," the boy said.

"That's a funny name for a boy," Amarine said.

"Is it?" Pic asked in an older, more familiar voice. Then he smiled. His mouth was full of needle-thin teeth.

Amarine helped Pic to bed by the hearth, tucking him into the blankets, ensuring he was comfortable and warm. Shai said nothing; her wife seemed unbothered by Pic's true nature, so Shai told herself the boy was safe. Afterward, as they lay curled together in their bed, Shai was restless. The events of the long night had left her feeling full of dread. And as she listened to the wet, soft sounds of Pic's breathing, that feeling only tightened its grip.

***

The fits started within the hour. Shai first found Amarine at the woodpile, standing still, axe held in her hand. Her eyes looking off to nothing, her grip on the axe firm, her feet planted into the ground. Shai shook her, kissed her, held her, whispered in her ear. She yelled at her, she pushed her, she slapped her across the face. But for an hour Amarine stood still as a carved wooden statue, taking time only to breathe and blink, and when she came back to herself, she did not believe an hour had passed.

Amarine did not know where she had gone, or that she had gone anywhere. "I was right here," she said. "Chopping wood for the fire."

"No, you had disappeared," Shai said. "Your body was here, but *you* were gone."

"Don't be silly. I have nowhere to go."

The fits continued. Amarine would be gone for ten minutes, or three hours. The day passed like this, and Shai did not feel she could leave her wife's side for a moment. As what would happen if Amarine disappeared while she was building a fire? Or taking a bath? This left Amarine perplexed and amused, asking what she did to deserve such close and loving attention. But each time Amarine had a fit, Shai was right there, to make sure she was the first thing she saw upon coming back.

Pic was to blame, of course, but only after blaming herself. And she did blame herself, as the boy was still in the cottage. Amarine refused to move him, saying he was as asleep and quiet as a stone.

The swamp fairy had promised her three stars, and Pic must have arrived on the second. Shai was a fool to think that these stars would work out in her favor and everything would go her way. Amarine's story came back to her—Shai thought she could do no wrong, and now she was paying the price.

Her mother had always said how the events of one evening laid out consequences for weeks and years, how what people did in life was never confined to a single moment. She had made that bargain with the fairy not considering anything at all, she only thought about what *she* wanted, and now she reaped the punishment. Amarine was being taken from her by minutes and hours, all because of a silly dandelion seed.

She crept out of bed that night and walked out past the freshly tilled soil of Amarine's new garden. The frog song covered up all sound, and the forest canopy was so thick it was dark and black as far as the eye could see, as it was every night. But tonight there was a light, twenty paces out. A lantern. Someone had found them.

"You there," Shai said. "Who goes there?"

"I told you I knew where you were hiding," Baelin said. She stepped out, her face illuminated. "Your mother died here. Our fathers died here. Now you will too."

"I did not know," Shai said. She took a step back toward the log pile, toward the axe.

"You were too young. But Yann knows, he remembers, of course he remembers."

"So you've come to kill me now?" She took another step back; she would only need a few more to reach the axe. "Kill me before you take Amarine. I cannot bear to see you take her away from me." But Baelin wasn't following Shai back toward the log pile. Moving further was too risky, it would leave the front door exposed, and then…and then Amarine would be gone forever. No, Shai would have to do this another way—she would have to play Baelin's game.

"What do you want, Baelin?"

"Retribution for my father's death," Baelin said. "And I will have it." She turned around and opened her hand, blowing across it to scatter some dust behind her that got carried away on the breeze until it eventually escaped the light. "That was your scent, which I stole from your cloak last night. Now Yann's hounds can track you across the water. I will bring him to you, just as I promised."

"Your mother taught you well," Shai said.

"And yours taught you nothing." Baelin lifted the lantern higher, looking over Shai's shoulder. "Pity for you they always pick the wrong women."

"When will my brother come?" Shai asked. "You can tell me that much."

But Baelin shrugged and then everything went dark. Shai lunged forward at the spot where Baelin had stood, but there was nothing left. The only light left came from the dwindling hearth inside the cottage; there was no splash of footsteps, no clamor of horse hooves. Baelin had disappeared as quietly as she had come, and now she'd left a trail for the hounds to follow. Yann would be coming soon; the danger was too near. She and Amarine had to leave.

Shai hurried inside to pack provisions. They would flee the cottage tonight.

***

Shai was gathering food and water when the door behind her flew open. She whipped around, catching Amarine and Pic rushing out of the cottage, laughing and holding hands. Shai followed them, leaving everything behind, the food, the water, the cottage. She rushed out to the edge of the swamp to see them disappear into the dark. She could only hear their footsteps playing in the water, then sludging through the muck, then leaping over tree branches.

She would kill Pic for this, fairy or not. She wrenched their axe from the wood block and ran off into the swamp. When her feet hit the cold water, she didn't stop. Amarine's laughter pulled her forward through the dark. She ran as she had run to Amarine every time they met secretly in the swamp. She ran as she had run to the cottage fearing Yann's retribution, Baelin's warning, the town's fury. She ran with both fear and worry driving her forward to the sound of Amarine's footsteps. As love had driven her before, love drove her forward again.

Amarine and Pic were running so fast, so easily, while Shai struggled for every step she took. The axe's weight was heavy but she refused to let go. She had to climb over tree branches, fighting the weight of her soaked boots and skirts. She often fell into deeper water and every time would pick herself up, hearing their footsteps even further away, their laughter too distant not to be a memory. Her breath was wet in her chest and her heartbeat was loud in her ears.

Soon, too soon, the swamp sounds drowned out Amarine's laughter, her footsteps, Shai's hope. She heard Pic's laughter crescendo before she caught sight of a will-o'-the-wisp. Shai called out to it, "Stop! Please!" And then it was gone, and she was alone.

The swamp fairy had promised that she and Amarine would be married; that was all Shai had wished for. Now Amarine had been stolen from her, and Shai had nothing. She sunk to her knees in the water, drawing the axe across her lap; all her hope had gone.

If I stay here, I can become part of the swamp, she thought. *As much of it has become part of me.* Two nights before her mother had run off, she had kissed Shai on the forehead and said, "You will always be my special star." It was the last good memory Shai had of her. She searched her memories for the last one of Amarine, but she couldn't find one. She was empty. She couldn't cry. She couldn't move.

For years Amarine had loved her. They met secretly, but Shai wanted more. She had ruined it, she had been selfish, she hadn't considered anyone else's wants but her own. Now Amarine was gone, lost, and Shai was lost. Sinking into the swamps to be swallowed by them forever.

Too soon.

Hounds bayed in the distance, and with them came the sound of splashing feet. The mob had come for her, and they would find her here—a broken shell of a thing, an empty piece of what she once was. No, she wouldn't let them have that.

Off in the distance there was a light of a will-o-the-wisp. There. There she would make her last stand. Shai was her mother's daughter, and she would die as she imagined her mother had, fighting to her last breath. She started running, and the dogs picked up pace. Their howling was getting louder, and the footsteps were coming closer. They had her scent; they would take her down.

She sped up, fighting against the weight of everything that tried to hold her back. She ran for her mother, she ran for her father, she ran for Amarine, and she ran for herself. She ran until her breathing choked her, until she fell more times than she stepped forward. She ran until she was crawling, until she was coughing, until she was shaking. She would die before she reached that light, but at least she would die knowing she hadn't given up. She would die with pride still in her.

When her muscles seized and her throat was lit with fire, she stopped moving, hearing the crash of footsteps closing in. As she lowered herself into the water, she felt lighter. She forgave herself for not saving her mother, for not stopping her father. She allowed herself to love her brother and his want to protect the town, to protect her. She forgave herself for her wish, and her want to love Amarine. And she allowed herself to believe that Amarine was safe, safer than she would be with Yann, safer than she would be with her or anyone now. She let go of her regret, her self-doubt, her hate, and when it was all gone, she knew she could die.

At peace with herself, she closed her eyes to sink deep into the cold when someone lifted her up from the mud.

"Be still," the swamp fairy said.

The fairy's fingers closed like a vice on Shai's shoulders, her black eyes fathomless. Shai tried to pull away, but there was nothing of her left.

"Shh," the swamp fairy said, setting her down. In her hand, she held a single dandelion puff. "Make a wish, but choose carefully."

Shai had lost everything she had and everything she wanted to one wish, so what would the cost of one more be? As the swamp fairy cradled Shai's head and neck in her webbed fingers, Shai thought of something she hadn't considered: Why? Why grant *her* wish? Why turn Yann against her? Why take Amarine away?

But Shai was too weak, so all she could say was: "Why?"

Yann's voice in the distance called for everyone to close ranks, and there was torchlight shining off the water. The hounds were so close that their pursuit had become the padding of soft dog steps. Through all this, the swamp fairy stood in front of Shai, her swamp-weed wings hanging heavy on her back, her skin shimmering.

"Hurry," she said. "We do not have much time."

What did Shai want? She wanted Amarine back. She wanted the mob gone. She wanted to be in love as she had been these past few weeks but before as well. She wanted her brother gone. She wanted Amarine's family alive. She wanted so much. Too much.

She could hear Yann clearly now. "Torches high," he said. "Weapons at the ready."

Shai closed her own hand around the swamp fairy's and looked into her black eyes.

"I wish," she said. "I wish I had the power to undo all that has been done to me."

And she blew the seeds away like stars, and fell into darkness.

***

"Is it her?" Yann asked.

"No," Baelin said. "It isn't. Don't touch it."

Shai opened her eyes and stood, and the men fell back, holding their weapons higher. Their torches were stuck fast in the mud. When Shai took a step forward, she felt unsteady, her arms and legs loosely connected, her body reacting in a swerving, drunken way. Her mind was agile and crisp. She assessed the threat: thirty men, no, fifty, all with swords, axes, or pitchforks, and she was unarmed and free of fear.

She looked down at her sallow-green slick hands shining in the torchlight. She saw her naked legs, her bare feet. Her body knew what to do without her; her wings extended, sending several men to their knees, but Yann and Baelin stood firm.

"Stand down, fairy," Yann said. "Tell us where the witch went."

He did not want the answers he would get, and he was not asking the right way. So she took a clumsy, snake-like step toward him. Yann raised his sword higher, Baelin moved forward. The poor fools, they were only making this worse for themselves.

"Tell us," Yann said. "Or die."

Shai smiled her response. She did not have to answer Yann's question, for the first time in years. She did not have to tell him anything. She had her family with her now, and they were close, closer than he'd ever been with her. They were behind her, around her, rallying with her. As she reached out to put a hand on his shoulder, he swung his sword, but her movements were quick, darting. She closed her fingers around his throat.

"Yann, there's more," Baelin said. "Three more...no, four. Five...six. We're surrounded."

She stumbled back and was snatched high up by the shoulders.

"I've come for Amarine," Yann said. "I only want to take her home."

"But, brother," Shai said. "She is with me, and we are home."

And she extinguished the torches, plunging them all into the black swamp night.

***

The mouths and lungs of twenty men filled with water that night. They drowned in a melee of fists and wings, of screeches and cries. The dogs remained placid, silent, eventually making their own way home. Yann was among the twenty, buried in the muck like Shai's father, who had come for her mother so many years ago. Baelin, too, was lost—she had never been as clever as her own mother. The thirty that remained hurried home when dawn broke, when the rooftops of town were silhouetted against the sky.

As the sun filtered through the trees and shone off the swamp pools, Shai and Amarine claimed one as their own. They dipped down beneath the water together and saw a world made of starlight and wishes, of potential and emotion. A world where love was so real, it was singing. Shai took Amarine's hand in hers, their webbed fingers winding together, their onyx black eyes fixed on the wonder before them.

While they stood, their wings at rest, Shai felt Amarine's heart beat in harmony with her own while the scene played out before them in flashes of light and color, both familiar and overwhelming. Like when her mother and father would laugh in the kitchen while she and her brother fought at the table. The house then smelled of warm fires and her mother's cooking, and there was nothing ever but happiness there.

Like when Amarine first kissed Shai on the long road by the Keep. Her eyes were so bright green and curious, and her lips were as pale as her skin; she looked as perfect as a drawing. And Shai reached out with her own soft hand and stroked Amarine's hair for what she wanted to be forever.

Shai held Amarine's hand tightly in hers as she stepped forward—this was what she'd always wanted, for her, for Amarine, for the both of them. She was surrounded by mothers and brothers, by fathers and sisters, by lovers and paramours, by all the magic in the world, and love. Love to give, love to receive, love to offer to the world freely, and Shai could feel it welcoming her and Amarine in.

This was where they belonged. She touched Amarine's forked tongue with hers, ran her needle-thin teeth along Amarine's lips, and it was like this that they tumbled down through the waves of magic, through the starlight, until they arrived finally home.

The Hollow Tree

There are two kinds of secrets: those we keep from others, and those we keep from ourselves.

My mother told me this after one of her too-silent nights with my father. She told me that the worst ones, the ones too terrible to believe, are the second kind. She told me she hoped I'd never have one of these kinds of secrets, as she leaned over and kissed my forehead. Only then did she go to her bed. Three days after that, my second sister came out of her, unbreathing. That time, she did not cry.

She told me, "Pira, you won't cry either."

She told me, "Pira, you have to be strong for me. I need you to always be strong."

And so I was.

I was strong every day as my father served my mother's pies through our bakery window, telling all our neighbors in Stowe that they were his. He smiled through his thick black beard, dripping with sweat and grease, joking with each person who came by each day. My father's smile was a smile I had grown to hate. But the town hadn't. They always said: "Silas Baker has such a wide smile to go with his sad eyes." They always said: "There are no pies sweeter than Silas Baker's pies." They always said: "He must make his pies so sweet for his lost daughters."

Every day, my mother made the pie fillings while I made the crusts. And every day, my father would sell the pies, his smile never tiring. Every evening, my mother and I would clean the kitchen. She scrubbed her knuckles raw on the oven bars and wood counters while I stayed on hands and knees cleaning the floor and cupboards.

My father spent this time in the back rooms in front of the fire. He had his favorite mug in his hand; he sat in his favorite chair. Every evening, when we were done, my mother would go to fetch him for inspection. And every evening, he found something wrong. Every night, they retired to our room to too much silence before I was allowed to join them. When I did, the room smelled of sweat and felt too crowded, although my mother had already left to go tidy her mistakes.

I was welcome in Stowe, where I ran errands for my parents. I had friends, like Elias, the tailor's boy, and I was friendly with other shopkeepers in town. I knew the layout of the farms and the orchards. I knew about the woods and their guardians. I knew about the legends they held. My mother had told me some, my friends had told me others, and I had gone exploring for more on my own.

Stowe was interested in me the way I was interested in all of them. I was interested in everyone's tidy lives, in their clean faces, in their happy hellos. All the while, the town whispered about me: "When will Silas find her a husband?" Or they whispered to me: "When will you get married, young lady?" Sometimes they told me: "It's time for you to be thinking about a family of your own." But I had my mother to protect, because she needed protecting.

My father never had guests over to our back rooms the way my friends said their families had guests over. We were a solitary family, aside from my father's friendliness at the bakery window. As my mother had told me, we had secrets to keep from others—written all over my mother's face.

One evening, close to my eighteenth birthday, my father inspected the kitchen and found a raisin on the oven door. He plucked the raisin off, set it on the clean and oiled wooden counter, and took my mother back to our room. I couldn't bear another few hours of silence. My mother needed protecting, but I knew not to interfere. So I took the raisin in my fingers, dropped it into my dress pocket, and hung my work apron and bonnet by the door.

I wanted my mother to be safe. I wanted my own life. As it was now, I would never get either.

A friend had told me of a fairy in the wood that liked to meddle in humans' affairs. He told me, "Your needs have to be dire, and the price has to be right." I closed my fist around the raisin in my pocket and walked out into the empty Stowe square.

***

I was long past the town gates, running along the cornfields on Anson Farmer's land. Their green stalks towered over me, heavy with corn, ready for harvest. Cornsilk hung down long, tangled, and golden like my mother's hair. Anson Farmer's cornfields bordered the woods I wanted, with the fairy I wanted. But he was also a gossip, one I would normally be wary enough to avoid.

But tonight I was too determined. In my flight from my father's house, I could think of nothing else but the fairy and my mother's salvation. I did not think of what my father might do if he found me missing. I did not think of what Anson Farmer might think of me traveling along his road at night. I did not think. So I did not look for him. As I ran past his house, I did not notice whether he was awake; I did not notice whether he saw me.

Anson Farmer's road led right to Stowe Pond, where Pastor Laeren did his baptisms and where Elias Tailor liked to go night fishing. Elias and I had met here several times in the ten years we'd known each other. At one time we would go exploring around the woods together. But that stopped two years ago, when his mother found him a girl to marry and my second sister was lost before she was born.

I needed Elias now though. Tonight. Elias was the one who had told me about the fairy I now wanted, so he was the one who could tell me a little more.

It was a cloudy night, and the moon was only a slim crescent, so the road was dark, the leaf-dotted path to Stowe Pond even darker. The path was underneath Anson Farmer's apple orchard, and I had to be careful so as not to slip and twist my ankle on a fallen apple. So I slowed, stepping on twigs and being too loud—so loud even the crickets noticed and stopped singing at my approach.

Elias Tailor noticed my approach as well, from his usual fishing spot at the bank of the pond, his posture perfect—too perfect for a fisherman—and his clothes fitting him neatly, as a tailor's son's would. He pulled in his line when he recognized me, but his face was written with concern.

"Pira," he said. "I'm happy to see you, but does your father know you're out here?"

"No," I said. "He doesn't, and that's rather the point."

"I don't want you to get in trouble. What are you doing out this late?"

"Looking for you, first," I said.

He didn't blush. He only blinked. He never blushed around me once, not ever. He never blushed around girls at all.

"You found me," he said. "What are we up to this time?"

"I want to go to the Hollow Tree," I said. "And you know the way."

"I do know the way," he said. He knew we were up to something. He had a sly way of speaking when we were conspiring. "Do you know what you want?"

"I do," I said.

"You only think you do." He picked up his rod and tackle. "That's the trick."

We walked past the pond and deeper into the orchard. Elias led the way, cutting between the trees so that we trailed along the cornfields again. I reached up and touched the cornsilk as we passed. I only wanted to touch it, to think of my mother, but pieces of it broke off in my hand. I pretended this was not a bad omen. With all the talk of fairies and the Hollow Tree, I hoped this was not a curse. I prayed it was not a curse.

I put the broken pieces of cornsilk in my pocket with the raisin and kept walking, saying nothing. Elias said nothing either. He asked no questions about the Hollow Tree. He said nothing about my father. But people with their own secrets do not ask about the secrets of others.

The smell of the orchard made me thirsty, and the air was heavy, like it had just rained or was about to. I did not take any apples, as I used to when Elias and I once played in this orchard. I did not pocket any other treasures. I was older now. I had my father to think about. And Elias had obstacles of his own.

The Hollow Tree stood on the border of the cornfield and the orchard, looming over Anson Farmer's land. The rumor was that Anson Farmer had made a deal with the fairy here, which is why his crops grew twice as tall and twice as abundant as his neighbors'. It was also why he was twice as mean. The town always said: "He dabbles in black magic." The town always said: "He consorts with fairies." The town always said: "He's evil." But they bought his corn and his apples and his cider and delighted in every bite and sip.

The closer I got to that hulking black mass of trunk and naked branches, the colder I felt. The night seemed to darken, the air felt as if it was even heavier, but Elias still approached—so I did too. The stories about the Hollow Tree were only stories. Stories about black magic. Stories about things gone wrong. As Elias had once told me, *The need had to be dire*. And mine was. I knew what I was going to say; I knew what I wanted. What the need was.

But I did not know how it was going to play out. How could I know that?

Mushrooms grew in a semicircle around the base of the Hollow Tree, scattered and haphazard, tall and wet and earthy smelling. The trunk yawned open, split by age. The tree stood black, cavernous, and uninviting. All of the Hollow Tree was uninviting—nothing grew on it. No leaves or lichen. No fungus or flowers. No birds even came to roost in its barren branches.

The tree appeared dead, but those of us in Stowe knew better.

"You have to knock three times on the trunk," Elias said. "And then whisper what you want to the bark."

"What about my gift?"

"That comes later," he said, and placed a hand on my shoulder. "Remember, Pira. The fairy doesn't give you what you ask for, she gives you what you want. So try to make them the same thing."

He then stepped back, standing a respectful distance away as I went up. I knocked three times, the sound shaking the branches above. I leaned in to whisper, my breath brushing the dry bark.

"Please," I said. "Please make my family happy again."

I walked away, wanting to stand next to Elias, but he gently urged me forward, away from him. So I stood alone. Waiting.

I waited some. And then I waited some more. I thought nothing was going to happen; I was certain of it. But then there was a shift in the air. The earthy smell of the mushrooms grew stronger, and the smell of the apples drifted away. Then the dew shook off the mushrooms. That was how I knew the fairy heard my request. The Hollow Tree groaned loudly like a wounded deer, and its branches twisted and turned. I was about to run away when the yawning trunk snapped shut, and then it opened, with the most curious person standing inside.

She was as tall as my hips and had toothpick legs that rose all the way to her breasts. Her hair hung down in black strings over long arms that bent at her knees. Her fingers were pointed, but not threateningly so, and they stroked her too-long chin as she approached.

"You bother me for happiness?" she asked. Her black eyes were narrow. Her voice, unkind. "You wake me for happiness?"

"Yes," I said. Now was the time to be afraid.

"I have punished people for much less things," she said. "Should I wake up and grant each person happiness, what would I be? What would this place be?"

"But you granted Anson Farmer great gifts," I said.

"He did not ask for *happiness*," she said. "And he came to me truly suffering. You are not suffering, little girl. But you will yet."

"She is suffering," Elias said. He was still standing behind me, still holding his fishing pole. "Tell her, Pira."

The fairy's head snapped from Elias back to me, and she smiled. Her teeth were all rounded, like pebbles.

"Speak," she said. "Tell me how you suffer. There may yet be a bargain tonight."

"My father, he hurts my mother every night," I said. "She cannot see anyone due to what he does to her face. He gives her tasks, duties, and she does everything he asks, everything he wants. Yet he still hurts her."

"Go on," the fairy said.

"I had two sisters," I said. "They both died before they were born. My father is to blame, for what he does to her. I'm afraid he might one day kill her. I fear I can no longer protect my mother."

"And you?" she asked. "What do you gain from all this?"

"He has not yet found a suitor for me," I said. "I cannot live my own life until my mother is safe."

"I believe I can make your family happy again," the fairy said. "But it depends what you have in trade."

I pulled the raisin from my pocket, and then, after thinking for a moment, also pulled out the pieces of cornsilk.

"I have for you the token of my father's rage," I said, giving the fairy the raisin. "And a symbol of my mother's hair." And I gave her the cornsilk.

"This will do," the fairy said. "When I leave, wait for the Hollow Tree to bestow you with a gift. Use it to make your family happy."

"Thank you," I said.

"Ah, but I am not done," she said. "I require something from you. When you have made your family happy, you will have to return to me with a token of that happiness. Only then will the bargain be fulfilled, because only then will I have my gift. My assurance."

"Of course," I said.

"It is done."

She retreated with my gifts back into the Hollow Tree. With another shiver and groan, the trunk snapped shut, swallowing her up. When it opened again, there was something there. I went to retrieve the item and recognized it immediately. It was my father's favorite mug.

The mug was exactly his, down to the chip on the handle from when he fell asleep with it on his knee and dropped it; down to the worrying on the lip from where he always rubbed it with his thumb; down to the bottom, where etched were the words: "Love, Lunan."

Lunan was my mother's name.

"Did you get what you asked for?" Elias asked.

I showed him the mug, and he looked at it, and then looked at me.

"I think you got what you wanted," he said.

"What I want is for my mother to be happy," I said. "I don't know how this is supposed to make her happy."

"Well," Elias said, "maybe that cup is supposed to poison your father."

People with their own secrets are very good at guessing the secrets of others.

***

I arrived home, and my mother was waiting for me by the hearth. The fire was long dead, the sound of it replaced by my father's snoring. My mother's hands were folded across her hips, and her eyes were wet with worry.

"Where were you?" she asked.

But before I could answer, she grabbed my wrists. "I lost two daughters before they could draw breath. I will not lose my only living one."

She brought me into her arms and held me close, her whole body shaking, her tears mingling with mine. My hand was still holding the replica of my father's favorite mug. I held her back tightly, mug and all; I held her back as if the mug had done its magic and all her horrors were all over. I held her bruised face to my chest and ran my hand over her tangled hair.

I whispered to her while I held her there. I whispered to her over and over again.

"I'll make it better soon, Mama. I promise. I promise."

***

The next morning, before my father woke, I replaced his favorite mug with the replica the fairy had given me. I hid the real one under my bed among the toys I no longer played with; the toys my mother had made me keep for my future sisters. As my mother and I cooked breakfast, I watched her pour my father's tea into the fairy's mug and bring it to him in our room.

The rest of the morning, I was distracted with anticipation. My father had his usual three mugs of tea; neither he nor my mother noticed anything odd about the fairy mug. My father said nothing about the tea other than his usual morning banter. He said, "My, what a gloomy day it is." It was true; it was gloomy. He said, "I'll need to fetch milk again." It was true; he would. He said, "Pira, you look very sleepy today." It was true; I was sleepy. As he spoke and as he swapped his tea out for water, I checked constantly for signs of poisoning—slurred speech, cloudy eyes— but my father remained smiling and talkative as ever.

He was at the window as he always was, his beard greasy and black. His smile wide for all the customers. If my father was indeed poisoned, he showed no sign of it.

Anson Farmer came by in the late afternoon. He bought a blackberry pie with blackberries from a neighboring farm.

My father said, "Anson, so good to see you. How's the harvest coming?"

"Truth is, Silas," Anson Farmer said, "I'm not here for the pie. I saw your daughter with the Tailor boy last night. Might want to keep a leash on that one."

"My daughter?" My father turned and winked at me. I checked his eyes; they were not bloodshot.

"He's spoken for, Silas," Anson Farmer said. "They were on my land and then disappeared. I'd keep an eye on your Pira."

"Thank you, Anson," my father said. "You're always looking out for me."

My father hovered around me for the rest of the day, checking my crusts, commenting on my work. He said, "My, these crusts are flaky, Pira." He said, "Roll that dough down flat, that's my girl." He said, "Very nice crosshatch." My mother attempted to intervene, but there was nothing she could do. Perhaps because my father was a large man, his chest round and thick like a boar's and his temper just as brutish. Or perhaps because I was hovering around him so that I could smell his breath as he leaned over me. But I found no smell of rot or death on him; no evidence of poisoning.

The fairy's promise had gone all wrong. Had my bargain been for nothing? Had I failed to save my mother? Had I failed to save myself?

When my father locked up the window for the night, my mother and I set to cleaning, and she cleaned again what I had cleaned. She cleaned it twice as hard. I knew what was coming. My father had turned his attentions on me.

He came in, carrying the fairy mug, and set it down on the counter. This time, he inspected everything, which was twice cleaned and three times as well-done. But he went over with extra care, feeling, sniffing, even tasting his fingers, all while watching me.

"These floors," he said to me. "They're sticky."

They weren't. They were smooth and waxed and I could see my reflection in them.

"Pira, it's your job to clean the floors, isn't it?"

"Yes, Father."

"Come with me," he said. And his hand closed around my wrist, and my stomach twisted around myself, and I felt my whole body go cold. I had trouble swallowing as if I was trying to swallow all my fear, all the coming pain. I was as weak as a rag doll, and as simple. I stood at the counter, staring at my father; all I could see was him, and all I could hear was: "No!"

Before I could move. Before my father could take me anywhere, there was a flash of red, then white, like a match strike. Followed quickly by the crunch of teeth on bone. My father's black eyes rolled back into his head, and he swayed to the right, then the left, and then crumpled to the floor. My mother stood beside him, the fairy mug in her hand burning white-hot as my father's blood spilled out over the clean, waxed floor.

***

My mother and I each accepted a lock of my father's hair at the funeral, as was custom. She held hers in her hand, and I put mine in my dress pocket, closing my fist around it as Pastor Laeren spoke to us and all of Stowe about the legacies of great men. As my father was lowered into the ground, my mother did not cry. I did not cry either.

Anson Farmer came up to my mother and held her hand once it was all over. "Terrible accident," he said to her. "If you need anything, Lunan, just ask."

The town was abuzz with my father's death. Silas Baker was a much-loved man in Stowe, but he was also a curious man. The town said: "What a tragedy for his wife and daughter." The town said: "Did you see Lunan Baker's face?" The town said: "Pira must be so afraid." But my mother and I were no longer afraid. We were relieved.

The night after the funeral I met Elias Tailor at Stowe Pond and we returned to the Hollow Tree. This time I did not care if Anson Farmer saw. This time I did not care what Anson Farmer thought. Elias and I walked to the Hollow Tree and I held the lock of my father's hair in my pocket, running my fingers across it. This would have to be enough.

When we reached the tree, Elias said, "I know his death wasn't an accident."

I said, "I know you know."

And he smiled and looked at his hands. People who keep others' secrets often do not share their own.

I went to the tree and knocked three times. I whispered to the bark, "I have your happiness here." And then I stepped back beyond the mushrooms.

The air changed. The mushrooms shook off their dew. The Hollow Tree twisted and turned; it groaned like a mourning deer. Its yawning trunk snapped shut, and when it opened, the fairy walked out and toward me on those long, long legs. Her eyes were wide with anticipation.

"You have your token?" she asked.

I held up the lock of hair, and she accepted it with her pointed fingers. Her too-long chin was turned down as she inspected the black strands.

"This will do," she said. "In some time, I will share the token of my own happiness with you." She turned back to the Hollow Tree and stood in its cavernous trunk. "You will see. We will both be happy."

And with a shiver and a groan, the trunk swallowed her up, and she was gone.

***

Several months later, my sister was born. She had black hair like my father. Her legs and arms were long, and she had a pointed chin. The town said: "Lunan must be so happy to have something to remember Silas by." The town said: "What joy finally arrives at the Baker house!" The town said: "She looks a little odd for an infant." My mother asked no questions; she knew the stories of the Hollow Tree. She merely loved my sister and showed her all the joy she showed me throughout my life.

But over the years, things would go missing: combs, forks, toys. My mother and I knew better than to ask. As my sister grew, she would run off sometimes through the gates, down Anson Farmer's road, and past Stowe Pond. I would find her at the Hollow Tree, talking to the mushrooms, playing in the dew.

Each time I found her, I would take her home. We would leave the blossoming Hollow Tree behind. We would leave behind its birdsong and the gifts. Each time, I would wind my own fingers through my sister's too-long ones as we walked past Stowe Pond, past Anson Farmer's watchful gaze.

We held close to one another, my sister and I, and held close to our mother, as the town watched and gossiped and whispered that something was not right. We held close, because we had to. Because the town's talk had never helped us before. Because our secret was the kind to keep from others, not the kind to keep from ourselves.

Jewel of the Vashwa

I watched my love die in the claw of a Scorpion Man. I watched him sever her in half; watched as her long hair dripped down to the ground; watched as her hand let go of her spear; as her long legs folded under her; as the Scorpion Man's tail rose in triumph. His chitin carapace shone in the dwindling sunlight. So did my love's armor. Her armor that had served her so well until the end. Her armor that made her look like a queen, not a general. Many women had told her that. Many women.

Like me.

I knew when the Scorpion Man killed my love, when all his people charged forward at what was left of our sisters, that she had been right to send me away. I watched as the Scorpion Man's many charged our few, charged them across the flat desert sand. I watched this from my place high up on the red rocks of the Vashwa. I heard my love's own voice in my head, smooth and silky and dark as her hair.

She said, "Awanshe, you will live to tell our story."

And so, I will. I will tell it to all who listen. I will live while my sisters die.

What a terrible burden to bear.

***

But the truth did not happen that way.

That is only the truth I have told you before. Here is what happened. One truth for another. A story for a story.

***

The women of the Vashwa have always been at war with the Scorpion Men of the Ratch. And we have always loved them. We send our women to them and accept our women and our daughters back. We raise our chitinous daughters as our own, among our soft-skinned daughters, born of soft-skinned husbands, who come from other lands—softer lands, greener lands.

Your lands.

The Scorpion Men have always given as much as they took. They take our sons, we take their daughters. They take one of our oases, we snatch one of theirs. They destroy a caravan, we destroy a night patrol. We fall in love with one of their traders, and it is just the way of our soft-skinned women to love such a hardened man.

I, Awanshe, am a chitinous daughter. You can see my back and chest, made of segmented carapace. You can see it is as brown as my skin. My mother brought me home from her Scorpion Man lover, and she loved me as much as she loved my soft-skinned sisters and brothers. I was one of seven. Now I am one of five. When I came of age, I was presented with soft-skinned suitors, but I was a chitinous daughter and none of these soft men with their soft professions suited me.

I was a warrior. I fought with spear and spit. I had a venomous tongue and a dagger wit. My carapace hid not only the foolish fluttering of my heart, but the catch of my breathing. A chitinous girl could hide fear. Hide scars. Hide lies.

No, only a Scorpion Man would do. And he did do very well.

My lover, Tarkir, was tender, but he drank much and fought hard. We went to the bars in the Ratch every night and boasted and blustered our way through the melee until we came out breathing heavy and kissing hard. Tarkir's best friend, Kuvo, once said to him, "Stop playing with these boy-women like this Awanshe toy." And I said back to him, "I am more man than you are, Scorpion Boy. And I am more woman than you will ever have." The flat edge of my chitinous chest shone hard that night in the gaslights. The light cut against my segments; it cut harder against my wit. I felt Tarkir's dangerous tail wrap close around my leg then, as he pulled me into him.

Tarkir's claw always felt right on my back. His hand always felt right on my neck. His claw's weight had purpose. His fingers' callouses told stories. His touch told me he needed me. I explored his chitinous carapace with my own ten fingers, and his breathing responded as I wanted it to, as I hoped it would. It responded well.

Too well.

I spent a year with Tarkir in an attempt to do my duty as a woman of the Vashwa. But something was wrong. We spent every night tangled in each other's soft-skinned legs, tangled in the sheets, mouths on each other's mouths. We spent hours on top of one another. Behind one another. But still, no babies came.

When my queen demanded me back home, to fulfill my duties as a warrior, Tarkir took my hand in his. His hand was as brown as mine, our chitin matched in shade. But he was far taller, and his eyes wider and always full of wonder.

"I'll come for you," he said. "I'll come for you, Awanshe, Jewel of the Vashwa."

And we kissed again, for the last time.

I left him in the Ratch. I left all my memories of him in the Ratch. My carapace held Tarkir close to my heart. It also held my desire. It also held the truth.

Because when I returned to Vashwa, I found someone else.

***

Here is the truth I need you to believe.

Here is what I witnessed while standing on the red rocks of the Vashwa. Here is what I saw as the sun set on the flat desert sand. As night threatened to overtake us.

My love charged Tarkir with her spear held tight in her grip. Its dark wood shaking with each of her strong steps, her steel-leaf armor shining with every last inch of sunlight. Her eyes pierced Tarkir's soft soul. Her mouth writ in a sneer.

Tarkir rose up to strike my love down with his claw. His claw that had once held me so close. He rose up, tall as he was, mighty as he was. He rose up, and my love slid down into the sand. She slid into the sand and thrust her spear up. Up in and between the segments of Tarkir's chitin carapace. Up into and piercing Tarkir's soft and tender heart.

Tarkir died on that spear. He died with his lips coated in his own blood. Those lips I had once kissed so many times. Those lips that had told me they loved me. My love threw Tarkir to the side, and the rest of my sisters, all the rest of them, charged forward across the flat desert sand. All of our many against Tarkir's few.

I knew, when we charged, that my love was right to send me away. I heard her voice in my head, dark and silky and smooth as her hair.

She said, "Awanshe, you must go to tell of our victory."

And so, I will. I will tell it to all who listen. I will live while Tarkir and his brothers die.

What a terrible burden to bear.

***

But that is not the truth either.

You must think me a terrible woman, to keep spilling lies forth again and again. To keep hiding the truth. Why do I do it? Because the real truth is too brutal. Honesty, too harsh.

***

I returned from the Ratch lovelorn and lovesick. A carapace is not as hard as steel-leaf armor. It does not protect from heartbreak. That wound slid deep, burrowing between my segments, eating me alive from the inside. So I returned to the Vashwa hungry and in pain. I returned longing for another's hands on my neck, another's mouth on my mouth.

I tumbled through temporary lovers. Chitinous girls and soft-skinned men, but none of them remained longer than a week. None of them remained longer than a few nights in my bed. None of them, until I took my place in the army; until I fell under our general's steel gaze.

Our general's name was Dalmana, and her hair was long—far longer than mine would ever be—and straight as a razor, while mine grew in curls tighter than corkscrews. Her hair was black like mine, her eyes were black like mine, but that is where our similarities stopped. Dalmana was short, far shorter than me, and had to bind her breasts to wear her steel-leaf armor. Her muscles rippled under her sweat, whereas my chest was chitin-flat, and my brown arms as sinewy as the acacia tree.

She first looked at me the way she looked at everyone, with disapproval, but it was the way her fingers trembled on my arm when she corrected my spear work that told me her heart. Dalmana's kisses tasted like wine and dates, unlike Tarkir's, which tasted like hops and salt. Dalmana and I spent our evenings drinking wine and eating goat cheese, looking out at her vineyard, and chasing her three chitinous daughters. At first, she was quiet and only talked of battle and training.

She told me how to be better: "Hold your spear like you're holding a man," she said. "Charge with your eyes everywhere, but always on your feet first. A prone warrior is a dead warrior," she said. "Our greatest asset is our sisterhood. Never forget that. Never," she said.

Dalmana told me plans of a new battle. One to take place soon. One she hoped I would be part of. I dreamed of this battle. I dreamed of it between her two older daughters bringing me candies and flowers. Her youngest daughter brought me a drawing she had done of me throwing a spear.

In truth, it was a drawing of her.

One evening, our legs wrapped together in the sheets, Dalmana told me stories of her life: where her children had come from, what she had been before she became a general, before she became a hero.

"Their father is the general of the Scorpion Men, Tarkir," she said.

My heart, long light for her, grew heavy and rough in its beating. It threw itself against my carapace. It rose to take hold of my throat.

"He called me Dalmana, Jewel of the Vashwa. We spent years together, to make my wonderful children. He was kinder to me than anyone before, or since." She stopped herself. "Except you, of course. You are my Awanshe."

"I didn't think I was included," I lied. I knew Tarkir was kinder, gentler, more affectionate than I would ever be.

"I will tell you a secret," Dalmana said. "But only you can know."

The soft spots of my carapace ached and shifted from the too many secrets I held already. I could not hold any more, but I would have to. For Dalmana; for Tarkir.

"Our next battle is not a battle, it is a truce. Tarkir and I are going to unify Vashwa and the Ratch."

"How?" I asked, but I did not want to know.

"You will see, my Awanshe. You will see."

***

Now we come to the truth of the battle; the truth I have held in for so long. It sits like a fever, burning deep between the segments of my carapace, eating me up from the inside. I must tell this truth to you, I must let it out. It is time I faced judgment for myself.

Tarkir and Dalmana have been judged for too long.

***

All two hundred of us stood on the flat desert sand, the red rocks of the Vashwa surrounding us, keeping us safe. We stood in the golden light of the late afternoon, our shadows long, as we stood with our weapons held ready, our armor laced tight. My sisters were hungry for bloodshed. I could see this by the way their tongues thirsted at their lips. I could see by the way they stood, by the way they hungered, that Dalmana did not tell them of the truce.

She had told only me.

Dalmana's gaze was cold, cast at the horizon. Her hand, too, was readied on her spear. Her armor, too, was laced for battle. I stood at her side, mirroring her posture, mirroring her gaze, as the Scorpion Men arrived. And as they did, my duty and Dalmana's truce festered inside me.

My Tarkir was at the front, his chitinous carapace brown and shining, recently polished. I imagined the feel of it underneath my callused fingers. I imagined the taste of his coconut oil against my tongue. He was smiling, his black eyes wide and bright and full of wonder. My heart grew as heavy as iron; it fell to my feet, and I became weighed down by it. My sisters continued to stand at attention, their shoulders back, their spears held at their sides. But my shoulders hung low, my spear loose in my hand.

My stomach was hollow with knowledge of this truce, of this peace.

Dalmana approached first, then Tarkir came to meet her under the boughs of a long-dead acacia tree. She called for me to join her, and my feet dragged through the flat sand. She gave me her knife and spear, to solidify the truce. Tarkir called for Kuvo, his right hand, to join him. Tarkir held his claw at rest, down at his side. Both Tarkir and Kuvo smiled in recognition of me, but it was Kuvo who took hold of my hand with a ferocity that shook my bones.

Then it began.

"Who proposes this truce?" Kuvo asked. His voice as confident as always.

"We do," Dalmana and Tarkir said together.

The truth will not let me deny it, Tarkir and Dalmana were harmonious in that golden light. All of them harmonious: their voices, their smiles, the way their eyes danced off each other. Tarkir held Dalmana's hand with a familiarity and a tenderness that he never had with me. With a love that I never had for either of them. Dalmana appeared truly at peace with Tarkir; her breathing was slow like the breeze. Her hair shone like his carapace, and visions of the two of them in his bed, on top of one another, behind one another, warred in my mind.

"In what way?" Kuvo asked.

Tarkir drew a line in the sand with his claw.

"This is the line that separates the Ratch from the Vashwa. It is the line that separates my love from my duty. I will not have them separated any longer. I will cross this line for love and duty because they are one and the same."

"No," Dalmana said. "*I* will cross this line for love and duty because, in my heart, they are both most needed."

Dalmana stepped over the line first, placing her hand on Tarkir's shining carapace. Her eyes did not leave his; his eyes did not leave hers. My grip was strong on my spear, as strong as Dalmana had taught me. My shoulders were back now, my eyes were on Tarkir's chest. I knew what had to be done. I knew what I must do for love and duty. I knew what was most needed for me, for mine.

Tarkir's right foot stepped over the line, his gaze locked on Dalmana. Kuvo stepped forward to protect Dalmana from the other Scorpion Men, his back facing me. Only my sisters could see me. And their eyes were all that I wanted, all that I needed. As Tarkir's tail passed the line, I stepped in front of him with my spear held ready.

He smiled at me.

"Hello, Awanshe, Jewel of the Vashwa," he said.

I said nothing. Instead, I lunged forward, thrusting my spear up and between the segments of Tarkir's chitin carapace. Up and in, piercing Tarkir's soft and tender heart. He was not smiling as his blood trickled out of his lips. His lips that I once kissed hard, kissed tenderly, kissed longingly. He was not smiling as he grabbed hold of my spear and looked at me with his black eyes wide, full of wonder, full of pain. I did not blink. I only thrust the spear forward again. I thrust it in deeper, in farther, and finally twisted it.

Killing him.

The hollow pit in my stomach was not sated as I threw Tarkir aside. It grew larger; my rage grew larger. It burned hot inside me as Dalmana grabbed my arm, her voice shaking, her body shaking. She screamed, "Awanshe, no!" I saw the pain written on her face. I saw the tears shining in her eyes. But I could not kill her too. My heart grew sick at the thought; it then stuttered as I looked down at Tarkir's paling face, at the blood flowing from his mouth.

I had done this, and it had done nothing to sate my jealousy. The emotion was still there, drowning me. The thunder of hundreds of footsteps was now coming for me, coming for war. This was what was most needed. This was my love and duty.

War for betrayal. Hate for hate.

I felt Dalmana's grip tighten on my arm, her trembling fingers this time spoke not of desire, but of fear. "Why?" she asked. "Why?"

But I would not say. I could not say.

I did not have to tear my arm away. Dalmana was torn from me by many of my sisters. They tore at her with their fingernails. They tore at her with their voices. They tore at her with their teeth, sating their bloodlust.

I was torn away by Kuvo. His bulk black and shimmering; his rage just as dark. Night was coming quickly; the battle would wear itself out before dawn. This I knew. So, as Kuvo swung his giant claw at my head, I ducked below it. As I ducked, I took a handful of sand. And when I stood, I blew him a kiss.

The sand flew into his mouth and eyes. He spat on it, choked on it. He screamed from the blinding pain. In his flailing, I jabbed my two spears into his soft-skinned leg and pinned him deep, deep into the flat desert sand. It was foolish to remain. It was foolish to stay where he could retaliate. Where he could recover and destroy me. So I left him there, writhing, cursing, and trapped.

I had only two knives to fight my way to an escape. To abandon Dalmana and my sisters. To flee. But I did flee. I did escape. When I reached the red rocks of the Vashwa, I could not look back. I only heard the sounds of death and slaughter below. I left my sisters behind. I left my love behind to go to her house; to take her food and her water; to kiss her daughters goodbye.

I vowed to make my own truth as I traveled to softer lands, to greener lands. To your lands. The truths that I have told you. The truths that all in this city and the cities that surround us now know.

Does the Vashwa still live? I do not know. Does the Ratch still thrive? Again, I do not know. I do not want to know. The truth is something I ran from long ago. The weight of it will kill me. I buried my emotions long ago. Tucked them underneath my carapace, let them fester like an old wound. The ghost of them now causes my old bones to ache with their memory.

Surely you can understand.

I have no daughters to carry on my stories, no legacy to live out the consequences of my lies. I have only this: that I, Awanshe, Jewel among Jewels of the Vashwa, killed all she loved that day on the flat desert sand. And that Awanshe, Jewel among Jewels of the Vashwa, has lived on a diet of lies ever since.

What a terrible burden to bear.

The Wind Whispers Secrets to the Sea

Our last husband was so hot, he burned the house down.

This was what we said to impress other women. We did not tell them of the firefighter's hands that night, so strong, so firm around our shoulders. "Are you okay, miss?" he asked, his voice, his voice like gravel. "You're so cold." We did not tell the women that our north wind had been acting up that night. We did not tell them that then, we were bitter, angry, powerful. That if pressed, we would have torn the whole neighborhood down.

We did not tell them of how we fanned our last husband's fire, his rage. How he drew from us all our energy—made us grow small, feel small. And then, when it became too much: a backdraft. We made our husband try to consume us, until he, himself, dwindled into the dirt.

The firefighter's hands on our shoulders were firm, heavy, laden. Stones. We knew that he would be too much. An anchor. We would tear him apart. Wear him down slowly, so slowly, until he was less of a thing.

"Do you have anywhere to go tonight?" he asked. "Anywhere at all?"

We answered him, our eyes blue and cold and beckoning.

We said, "No."

Of course, we went home with him.

***

These are the secrets we tell to the sea, as it draws us in, as it plays with our hands. These are the things we told to no one, to no one but the water. The firefighter had an apartment by the sea. He took us in, and we took him in. Afterwards he made a pot of coffee, it was bitter like we were that night, and we sat with its bitterness cooling in our hands, as we all watched the tide come in.

"What's your name?" the firefighter asked, far too late to be asking.

"August," we said. "What's yours?"

"My friends call me Cole."

Then he smiled. His teeth brown as wet sand.

"But what should we call you?" we asked.

Our north wind had settled back in the bedroom, between the sheets, sated by his weight, his steadiness, his grip. Now, now we were a precocious spring breeze, heralding storm. His smile grew wider. We saw that he liked it.

"You can call me this," he said, he said, and he leaned in.

Cole's lips tasted of the memory of our last husband. His tongue of hops and barley. His fingers of a man we could only erode.

***

We stayed with Cole two weeks, long enough to know how much he stayed close, was close. To learn how he settled, burrowed, into his chair when he returned home; to learn how much routine must be maintained. To learn the rhythms of his breathing, his chewing, his drinking.

We learned the secrets that the sea told us: that Cole spent his lonely evenings planting bottlecaps. That the sea had never seen him go through women, the way they knew we went through men.

You aren't right for each other, the sea said. *You'll eat him alive.*

And they were right.

They were right.

***

We left as insubstantially as we came, to protect Cole, to protect ourselves. We left with only the clothes on our back and fifty dollars in our pocket. We would find what we needed, what we wanted. We drifted; we traveled. We walked; we paid attention. We told the other women of Cole's hands, how they anchored us to the mattress. We told the other women of our last husband's heat, how we kept it burning all through the night.

We watched their eyes go wide. We fanned the flames of their desire. We let them take us home, to apartments with leaky faucets, to homes with more than one shower. We left sneaking out of windows, thrown out of front doors. We blew through the women who broke us by trying to hide us; we breezed past the women who thought we were broken—so then, we hid ourselves.

When our fifty dollars became fifteen, became zero, we found ourselves standing on the wet sand again, the color of Cole's firefighter teeth.

Hello, August, the sea said. *What secrets do you have for me today?*

"We're lonely," we said. "We're afraid that we will always be lonely."

But you're not alone, the sea said. *You'll always have me.*

"Will we always?"

Always.

"Then," we asked, our voice delicate as an echo, "may we join you?"

Their answer was simple.

Their tide came up to meet us. Came up to meet our toes. So we came up to meet it. And as we did, the sea's waves grew, and as their waves grew, our confidence grew. Their waves grew to swallow, swallow my hips, lick my fingers, caress my hair. This, this is what we wanted. To be adored. Not to be held down, and anchored. Not to be drawn in, and made small.

We wanted to be joined, joined as one together.

We dove under the water, we dove into the sea, into them. And their current, it took us in; the sea took our whole body in. They enveloped us, surrounded us. They brought us down into their body. And then the sea said to us, they said, *August, I love you. I will never, ever let you go.*

And the truth is, they never did.

They never, ever did.

The Black Hearts of La Playa

"There's no such thing as monsters, not really," Letty said to me once, pretending to shoot another starving lizard with finger guns. "I bet everyone's got a little monstrousness inside them."

I watched her holster and pull her finger guns as we sat on a pillaged picnic table, swatting locusts and sipping water. It was no secret I was in love with her. Me, Marrin Version 3.0. I'd been one version for my mother, another for Corporal, and now I was this version for Letty, the girl who liked to go shooting and give the wrong plots of old books as if she had read them dozens of times (when in fact she hadn't read them at all).

"Yeah?" I asked her. "What's your monster?"

She turned to me, hands on her knees, shoulders all serious.

"No, Marrin," Letty said. "I want to know about *yours*."

***

"Desert's got a vampire problem," Corporal said at the briefing later that night. "Letty, Marrin, you're on Eastwatch Tower detail. Nights. Don't get too distracted with...you know."

She smiled. 'Cause she knew. She'd seen me sneaking out of Letty's tent before, tying on my belt, fixing my hair. Corporal smiled then too, and lifted her chin, fixing her own hair. Like she did back when she and I were a thing.

The other Tower details got dealt out as Letty shot me a long glance across the mess tent, where we were shielded against the locusts that swarmed lights. Like everyone said: the insects would survive the apocalypse. Everyone was at least right about that.

What they weren't right about was most of the rest.

Once Corporal was finished and the socializing started, I stepped outside. Stepped out and down the ramp, out onto the asphalt. Camp was set up in what had been a parking lot, the abandoned vehicles cleared and scrapped decades ago for space and materials. There was a big building behind us that we used once, but, "We don't go in there no more," Corporal said to me a while back. "Roof keeps caving in on us. Don't got the means to fix it."

She knew me then; she knew me then like she knew me now. Knew I would come out here alone, 'cause I heard the wheels of her chair hit the ramp, then hit the asphalt behind me. I turned to find her looking up at me with that steel gaze that had fixed me to her long ago. Letty was still inside. She was a social animal; Corporal and I weren't, we never had been. We traveled solitary, or in pairs.

This remained, even when I was with Letty.

Or not with her.

Corporal was betting on this when she reached up and took my hand in a friendly, platonic gesture. Her blue eyes piercing through the haze of her safety goggles, her smile visible despite the scarf over her face. Still, gone was all the heat and immediacy of her movements. That desire that had pulled me to her, made me tell her the lies that I wanted her to believe about me. That I wanted anyone to believe.

"Careful with that one, Marrin," Corporal said. "Don't want you to go breaking her heart. She's a lot more fragile than me."

Corporal ran her thumb across the back of my hand, and then took off, glancing once behind her as she went. The memory of her kisses was hot on my lips: hard and fast, like she meant them as much as she meant everything. Letty's kisses were tentative, but her grip was sure. She always took me to her like I was the last kiss left in the world.

Me? I was desert silt: wispy and forming against either of them in a way that suited them, until they brushed me off. And both of them brushed me off: Corporal once, Letty more times than that. But like silt, I kept coming back.

***

Sun never rose anymore. In books it did, in stories it did, but not here. All the sun could manage to do now was edge over the horizon and light up this grey haze just enough to set everyone coughing.

I was already on lookout at Eastwatch Tower when the elevator shuddered behind me. Its shrieking doors opened to reveal Letty, all five foot four of her, dressed like me in dark clothing. Both of us with our bandoliers of wooden stakes, and gunbelts built for two six-shooter revolvers.

We wore scarves over our noses and mouths. Mine was a dull grey, colored that way from lackadaisical washing habits. Letty's was black on black, like the rest of her clothes. Like her hair. Like two of her teeth.

"I hate that thing," Letty said, motioning not to me, but to the giant gasoline beacon lighting up both our faces.

"Same," I said.

"Makes me smell like diesel for a decade."

She grinned at me, boots hitting the corrugated metal platform like her hyperbole. Letty was small, but she took up as much space as an argument. I had a weakness for women that overwhelmed me like this.

She grabbed my offered binoculars and looked at me, her face lit from the beacon firelight. Her face took on a softer quality lit up this way. Softer than when in the mess hall, in the haze of the day, under the fluorescent lantern in her tent. But Letty wasn't soft—there was nothing soft about her, from the callouses on the tips of her fingers down to the steel toes of her boots, she was all hard edges.

We were all hard edges anymore.

"Vampire problem," I said. "What else is new."

"It's Tuesday," Letty said.

True, but the days ran together now. Every day was Tuesday anymore.

***

Vampires struck in the late hours of the night, or the early hours of the morning, depending on one's point of view. My heart always struck at the same hours, reminding me of what I'd lost, what I'd given up, just to come here, just to be a part of this camp.

Letty had thrown me out of her tent three times, three times after three whispers of, "I love you, Marrin." Three displays of vulnerability, rawness so real she couldn't let me have it, hold it, or believe it. My belt struck my thighs with the same rawness, the same vulnerability, when she threw it at me.

"Get out," she also whispered to me. Three times.

My mother used to whisper poetry to me. Her own dangerous words of the sea, as I was named after people lost at it, wandering at it, the same way my mother wandered through her life. The same way I wandered through mine.

We often become our mothers, so the legends said.

"Marrin," my mother said so often, so much. "Listen. Stop squirming." And she would go on about her black and broken heart at the bottom of the ocean. Childless and free. And dead. It was too much for a child to bear, but I carried that heart in my pocket until she left me on the cracked and sundered sidewalk, left me to find my own way in this chaos.

A vampire knew its own way, so the stories said. They knew their codes and ways of being. They stayed to their communities tied to a morality so strict in antiquity there was no other way to be. It was almost romantic, if one still believed in romance. I didn't; the world was too dead for romance now.

Still yet, sometimes, late at night, I'd wander the desert beyond the shoddy camp walls, out of reach of the beacon lights. I'd wander with my bandolier and my revolvers—a safety net. But what I was looking for was anything but safe.

I was looking for a way out, like my mother did all those years ago.

I was looking for a vampire.

***

Letty kept the binoculars up, old heavy ones that showed off the thin musculature of her forearms. I leaned over the edge of Eastwatch Tower, peering out to the edges of where the beacon fire didn't reach. I was looking for a whisper of movement, a promise of action, but my own vision was clouded by the locusts and the scratches on my safety goggles.

By Corporal's orders, everyone wore these. Too many bugs.

Mine had so many scratches that they hid my expressions. With the scarf and the scratched safety goggles, Letty said they hid the truth of me. That the ugly parts that I didn't want anyone to see only came out in the harsh fluorescent light of her tent. Which is why she probably cast me out after whispering in my ear.

She never liked what she saw.

Letty brought down her binoculars and brought up her own safety goggles. They hid the mask of her. Made her dark eyes look softer, more innocent, which was the truth. Her vulnerability, her quiet tenderness, was what she wanted to hide from the world. Magnified by the scratches and blur of the safety goggles, now blinking back at me.

"Got one," she said. "There."

She passed over the binoculars and I took a look. Out in the darkness of the desert was a tall, lanky individual who looked too out of place for the desert. No scarf, no goggles. Sitting comfortably on an old vehicle uniframe in scuffed up boots and a long hoodie so holey it should take up religion. They were smoking a cigarette and looked like the sun hadn't touched them in years.

Totally a vampire.

"We should call in backup," I said.

"No need," Letty said. "We got this."

She'd already turned to call the elevator. Its bowels shook and ratted in its ascent, answering my own fear. The desert wasn't the only one with a vampire problem—Letty herself had one. Or more of an obsession. She had the highest vampire kill count out of anyone in Corporal's camp.

I had never killed a vampire, and Letty knew it.

"There might be more, Letty," I said.

"*There might be more, Letty,*" she mocked back at me. "Then bring them on, Marrin. We can take them." She fingered a wooden stake at my bound chest. "We can take them together. You and me."

And just like that, my heart skipped into my throat and I entered the elevator with her, our faces plunging into the orange safety lights, together.

***

Corporal had taken interest in me when I was patching asphalt. She wheeled up to me when my back and arms were all sweaty and said, "Take five, you. Can't have the new person getting worn out on their first day in camp."

I looked at her, her blue eyes piercing through her safety goggles, disarming me.

"I'm not new here," I said. "I've been here for three years."

"Well, well," Corporal said. "Then take five with me, old timer."

We cracked open beers and then cracked open memories. She'd inherited the camp from a man who'd inherited the camp from an old soldier, back when there were soldiers, back when there was civilization. She also inherited the title from him.

"What does it mean?" I asked.

"Dunno," she said. "But I like the sound of it. What the hell does Marrin mean?"

"It's short for Mariner," I said. "My mom liked stories about the ocean."

"Where is she now? Mom?"

I shrugged. She shrugged. Then we chugged our beers.

Some secrets have to be kept deep, deep in the drink.

Corporal said she liked me 'cause I had mommy issues, like her. I told her I liked her cause she took no shit, like me. But really I liked her 'cause when I was with her, I didn't ever have to second guess who I was or what I was. I was Marrin, Corporal's partner, and she held me to her so close it was like a secret kept deep, deep in the drink—one she never wanted to let go.

We were tight together, for a time. Corporal and Marrin, an item. Whispers went around the camp like a sandstorm, pitted and painful. They hit me harder than they hit her, or so it seemed. If Corporal was bothered, she only showed it in how much more she drank when we were alone, or in the looks that became more critical as we talked late and late into the night.

As she unraveled me, story by story.

Frown by frown.

I wasn't the person she wanted me to be. I was Marrin, the person with the mommy issues who came to camp looking for a place to belong and forget their life. I came to be alone and work; work myself into a community that would let me forget everything that had come before. Work myself into a community where everything, like surviving, was only forward.

Until Corporal. Until I fell into her needing me and she realized that what she needed *wasn't* me. Corporal needed someone who wanted a hero for a girlfriend. Someone who would let her save them from their wretched past, like some kinda knight. Still though, I couldn't be that for her, I still wanted her. I wanted the heat of her kiss, the grip of her hand around mine, the feel of her watching me from across the thoroughfare.

Maybe, though, I was wrong.

Maybe, just maybe, something in me *did* want to be saved.

'Cause when Corporal let me go, I hit the ground like sunset. Sudden, but with plenty of warning. I just refused to see it coming. The comments and whispers that came after dug in deep and necrotic, and I retreated more into myself than before. I had to find the source of these wounds, dig deep into what had turned me so wrong.

Had turned my heart to black.

***

It's easy to lose yourself in a person, the way the world lost itself in ending. Or at least people believed it did, for a while. And then we rebuilt and rebuilt and rebuilt. Generations later, we're still here: with greenhouses and protection from the bugs, living in tents in parking lots, taking shelter from collapsing roofs.

Like I said, the legends were partially true. Cockroaches and locusts are a constant reminder that we're just tenants around here. But the stories were mostly wrong. We've got chemists and botanists that engineer medication, and ramps and elevators and safety ropes 'cause they're just a good idea. People persevere. Despite what anyone ever said.

We've got wind power and batteries. We've got storytellers and history. We live despite everyone and every legend that told us it was impossible—even my mother. Like the locusts, like the cockroaches, we refused to leave.

There are only the skeletons of skyscrapers and sunsets and moonlight serenades, but we are more than that. We persevere as the meat and skin and breath of what is left by catching lightning bugs. With hot kisses out of reach of the beacon fire. With vampire hunts.

Like the one Letty and I are going on right now. And she's fifteen steps ahead of me.

***

Vampires hadn't changed much from before the world ended. Stories said they were still blood-sucking negative energy drains that thrived on destruction and hate. All they ever did was take, take, take (or so the stories said). They hung around camps like ours to disrupt us, to harm us. So we had to work to spite them. But mostly, because of them, we had to work together. Word was that vampire camps didn't work together, that they were sites of pure chaos, pure destruction.

But word and stories had been wrong before.

So much had been wrong before; it was hard to know what to believe.

Corporal's camp was this bright center of positive energy where everyone may not have liked their assignments or may not have liked their neighbor, but it was a society, and working to build and maintain the camp was how Corporal's society functioned.

"Don't like it?" she'd say. "Go join the vampires."

But bad people joined the vampires. Good people stayed in the camps.

Everyone said that.

I followed behind Letty as close as I could while she continued on her mission to break her ankle or break the sound barrier, whichever came first. I kept a torch up to try to light our path, smelling like diesel and old socks—'cause that's what I had on hand to make it. My heels blistered against my boots as I continued on, an excuse for my slow pace.

Letty's hands were shadows above the hilts of her revolvers. She was stalking ahead like it was high noon, closing in on our nemesis—her vampire, our vampire. They sat on the uniframe ahead, the cherry of their cigarette glowing intermittently in the black, quiet desert night. A quiet night punctuated only by the grit of our boots on the concrete, the scuttle of a leftover lizard, and then.

"Here for me, I assume."

It was them. The vampire.

"Hell yes, we are."

It was Letty. My would-be girlfriend.

"Well, let's get on with it," the vampire said.

They stood, finally illuminated in my torchlight. They were tall, as tall as me, with hair just as long and lanky. Their face was longer though, storybook long, with a nose that came down and hooked at the end. It stood in contrast to their wide, wide eyes that stared at me from across the expanse of Letty, whose revolvers were drawn and now pointed at our vampire prey.

"Wait," I said. "Wait a second."

"Why," Letty said. More of a bark than a question.

"Don't you want to know where they came from? If there are more of them? If they have a camp nearby? We need information."

"We don't need shit except this asshole dead."

"Dead-er," the vampire corrected. "My name is Aurin. And I am one of many, yes."

"See?" I said.

"How many?" Letty was seething. Her words hissing through clenched teeth.

"Very many," Aurin said. "But I didn't come for your camp. We don't want so much as all that. We're happy where we are; how we are."

"Then what do you want?"

Aurin looked at me. Their eyes still wide, wide and black as everything around us. Black as the ocean depths my mother wrote her poems about. Black as the wound that her leaving had left festering in me.

Black as my moods lately.

"I think they know," Aurin said.

And then they pointed at me.

***

The last time Letty had whispered that she loved me I had almost let myself believe it. Until she tossed my pants and my belt at me and told me to leave her alone, like she did the other two times. Taking that whisper and drowning it in her exterior machismo.

Earlier that night, when she was drunk and playing with my hair, she told me that she heard that there had once been flowers called buttercups, and white girls would hold them up to their chins to see if they were pure.

She told me she wanted to be pure.

When she pulled away, I watched her remove the dirt under her fingernails with the kind of precise hatred she reserved for broken glass on the thoroughfare, for locust moltings on her water bottle.

I told her she was pure. I lied. I lied to Letty all the time. I told her what she wanted to hear, because I wanted to be that person for her. She liked who I was when I did, wanted me around: a person she could hold hands with, spend time with, have in her company.

When I was me—when I wasn't lying—that's when she tossed me out.

That's when she mocked me.

Corporal wanted something I couldn't be, something I wasn't, and she let me go. It made sense—this was how relationships worked. But Letty—Letty wanted a piece of clay; she wanted desert silt. So for her I was the partner who let her be soft when she needed to be soft, who let her shine for her brief moments of vulnerability, and then let her close the door on me.

And I never complained.

Not to Corporal. Not to Letty. Not even to my mother when she read her sad, sad poems to me about never wanting to be a mother. Not even to my mother when she told me the whole world deserved to die, so we might as well all just let go.

I had been always not enough, or too much.

And Aurin knew that. That's why they'd come for me.

***

Letty's guns were still pointed at Aurin, still leveled straight at their chest with every inch of threat she had in her body. She was stoic rage, steel-toed boots planted into the desert gravel. But Aurin was unshaken by Letty's solid steel and gunpowder focus; they were looking only at me, their arm outstretched. Clipped, yellow fingernails pointing past Letty, past her shoulder, beckoning me to them.

"What you are, what you want, is with us," they said.

"No," Letty said, but her voice was unsure. As she turned her head back to me, her eyes were worried, lost behind the sheen of my torch in her safety goggles.

"It's true," Aurin said. "And they know it, unlike you."

"It's true," I said.

"So come with us." Aurin's voice was melodic, clear. Like wind chimes. "Come with us and leave all that you pretend to be behind."

I still held the torch in my hand. It still smelled of diesel and old socks. But the flame was waning and flickering in the dust and breeze of the late desert night. The dust which spat across the cracked and ancient road, across the crumbling sidewalks, pitted the dead trees, and probably collected itself in the carcasses of old buildings which stood yawning and open.

A danger.

"What else would I leave behind?" I asked.

"All that's behind you," Aurin said. "All that I offer is forward."

They smiled, showing two rows of pristine white teeth. Those teeth plus two perfectly pointed fangs. Lit up in the torchlight like this, they looked almost romantic, if I were into that sort of thing.

I wasn't, but it didn't matter.

Letty had turned her shoulders back to me now, her hands shaking, her resolve gone. Aurin was winning. And they knew it. They knew it as they stepped forward, pushing past Letty, pushing past her and placing a hand on my shoulder. Placing a hand on my shoulder and looking me directly in the eyes. I knew what they were going to do, and it worked, too, that mesmerizing gaze of theirs.

It totally worked, it worked like all the stories said it would.

Some stories, some legends, come true.

When Corporal had called it off, she sat across from me in her wheelchair, fingers clutching the last beer she and I ever shared. She was half-lit by her fluorescent lamp, her features cut to sharp edges by shadow. She was cutting me to pieces by words. Calling me callous, spineless, and (most accurately) over.

"Don't even think anyone'll ever know you, Marrin," she said. "Not like I did. Not like I figured you out. You're like one of them lizards, one of them that changes colors when it suits her. What's it called? A chameleon."

I nodded. I nodded and kept nodding, 'cause she was right.

Like I nodded as I took Aurin's hand in mine, lacing my warm fingers through their cold ones. I let them brush my hair away from my neck, something I had always thought would be sexy, but was almost procedural. When Aurin bit me, when their fangs pierced my skin, I heard Letty through a hurricane wind calling to me.

"Marrin, no. Marrin, stop."

But I was lost.

Or was I? 'Cause out of anyone I'd ever known—Corporal, Letty, my mother—out of anyone, Aurin was the only one who saw through my disguises right away. They saw through all my attempts at pretending. They saw *me*, they saw what I *wanted*.

***

While I was lost at sea in Aurin's embrace, as the tides of what was happening crashed over me, I remembered something Corporal said to me. I remembered something she said to me when I first came to camp. She said, "You're one a'them lost causes, ain'tcha?" She said, "If you're lookin' for something to believe in, you won't find it here, hon. You gotta find some way to believe in yourself."

When I hit the desert silt, I hit it fast as heartbeats. I had ten seconds of consciousness to watch Letty running toward me as I felt my last gasp of air leave my lungs. And then? I fell into the deepest, darkest sleep.

***

Four years ago, when my mother dropped me off on the road to Corporal's camp, she kissed me on the cheek and said, "Don't disappoint me, Marrin. I know you'll be good. Always be good." And then she brushed my lanky brown hair out of my face and looked me in the eyes. "I can't be good anymore. I'm done with it, and I don't want you to see that, my darling child."

I was twenty years old and not a child anymore, but still young enough to be betrayed by my mother. She walked away from me then, but I only knew that from the sound of her boots on the old, cracked concrete. There was no need to turn and watch her go; I walked forward, toward the camp gates, the four towers, and the beginning to someone else's story.

***

I woke some nights later alone on a cot underneath flickering sodium lights. My bandolier and revolvers were gone. So were my safety goggles and scarf. My body ached from disuse and death as I clamored to the concrete and slipped out of the empty, unfamiliar tent toward the sound of many voices, conversing in the dark.

As my new dead eyes adjusted, I saw Aurin, standing around faces I didn't recognize, but faces who turned to me as I exited the tent. So many faces, so pale, so curious. All smiling.

But I was me now. Not a counterfeit. So this time, I walked toward Aurin and all those faces. Again, with the same refrain. Aurin smiled, revealing their fangs, and a cacophony of applause rang out, coupled by a chorus of fanged smiles.

"Welcome, Marrin," they all said.

Aurin wrapped their arm around my shoulders. They turned me toward the assembled ease of the group. I leaned into their presence, I leaned into the chorus of fangs, I leaned into this version of myself.

"This is Marrin," Aurin said. "Join me in welcoming them home."

Personal Histories Surrounding La Rive Gauche, Paris: 1995-2015

I lost Lynne to the Seine. That's what I told authorities and the doctors and my friends twenty years ago after she disappeared. "I lost her." It was all I could say, after they all lay their hands on my slumped shoulder, looked me in the eyes and said, "She is gone, *chérie*. She lost herself. It is not your fault. It is time you lost her too."

So, I lost Lynne to the Seine, but that isn't the truth and I know it. The truth is that we were kissing under a streetlamp on La Rive Gauche twenty years ago. We were kissing and I had my fingers tangled in her hair that smelled like lilies and ashes. I could taste that night's tiramisu on her tongue and the just-flicked cigarette on her breath.

But just as she pulled away, and before she could take my face in her outstretched hands, she was snatched away from me. By a tall woman in a white coat with silver rings on each of her fingers. Snatched away and taken into the dark waters of the Seine, while still reaching for me. The tall woman's coat became silver fishtails, her silver rings stretched into webbing.

Those fishtails wrapped around my Lynne, the way my own legs would wrap around her in sleep, in not-sleep. The strange woman dragged her down, down into the darkness, and I watched, hand over my open mouth, as Lynne's mouth opened. As her hands reached for me, her eyes wide, the whites bright in the murk.

What did she yell down there in the deep? My imagination, my hope, says it was, "Victoria!" It won't let me have it any other way. My name, screamed in that way, echoes through nightmares.

Still.

***

Percy likes his tea like a good Englishman should, with milk and two sugars. So now I have it this way, because I don't have the heart to tell him that I like it black and mean, like an American. Every morning, he brings me my tea in the bath where I soak in jasmine bubbles up to my chin and we talk as if we haven't been talking for ten years.

"Bad night?" he asks with concern, even though he knows I had a bad night.

"Nightmares," I confirm, setting us both to nodding and sighing and smiling small English smiles where neither of us knows what to do. I know he felt me kicking in the bed last night. I know he woke up and said, "Victoria, shh. Shh." And I curled up in his arms where I'd learned it was safe.

"Paris?"

"Yes," I say. "Again."

What I don't say is, *Lynne, again.*

Because he doesn't like talking about Lynne. He doesn't like remembering my time in France with her, or anything about her. Doesn't like me mentioning how we lived, how we kissed, or particularly how she disappeared. "Oh, you know Victoria," he would say at parties where everyone wore silly hats to commemorate some holiday or another. "She had a *wild* past."

"What he means to say is, I'm bisexual," I replied, every time.

"She's from Paris," was his each and every answer.

Which is a lie, 'cause I'm actually from Minnesota.

"Right," he says now, as he always says. "A kiss should make it better. I should know, I'm a doctor."

We both smile as he places his kiss right between my eyes, while his undone tie splashes into the water as it always does, while he mis-buttons the top two buttons of his shirt, while his nametag hangs askew on his pocket. Announcing him crookedly as: *Dr. Percy Mantival, Psychologist, London Hospital.* Percy is a man who presents himself as a disheveled mess, but everything about him is calculated: every word, every gesture, every quiet shush.

All crooked in effect.

His kiss lingers, as it always does, washing away the lines trying to etch themselves between my eyebrows. The lines've made good progress. But Percy does his best every morning to hold them back.

When we actually kiss goodbye, Percy is sweet, like saccharine. He prefers berry scones and three sugars in his tea and anything with chocolate. Comedies to drama. Action comedies most of all. Percy says he loves to laugh. Lynne actually did, but it's easy to forget that sometimes. It's easy to forget so much sometimes.

"Best be off," he says, tying his half-soaked tie quickly.

"You'll be late otherwise."

"I'm always late," he says. "It's my aesthetic."

He dashes off into the wilds of the West Sussex commute and I stay inside as the smell of sugar hits my teeth before the reality of it can rot them. The smell halts me, as it has a habit of doing, causing me to simply hold the cup and stare out at the lone tree in the upstairs tenants' garden. It's budding.

It's spring.

***

Two months after Lynne was taken from me, I was in our shared St. Cloud flat, hardly living off of Gitanes and Nutella (a diet she would've been proud of), when I found one of her old poetry notebooks on the floor.

I leafed through it, about to cry. Again.

Instead, I stayed up all night. Stayed up until the dawn crept through the filthy windows and the traffic sounded the start of a new day. I didn't cry, because I was still stuck in yesterday's tears, stuck in weeks and weeks of grief. Reliving that time in this notebook, in its poetry, in its drawings.

Littered all over pages of this tiny notebook were crude sketches of those same two tailed mermaids. Ones that looked exactly like the silver-tailed woman who took Lynne away. Who drowned her? Looked exactly like the mermaid in the Starbucks logo: the one that drowns everything.

Reading through Lynne's poetry, I learned what *she* was, that silver-tailed woman. And what Lynne found so enchanting about her. About how this creature lived at the bottom of cold, cold waters, lived at the edge of men's curiosity. Lived with hungering need for the most beguiling and enchanting among all of us.

We women.

Among women, Lynne was always the most beguiling and enchanting. She didn't have to make an effort, she just was. Apparently, I was not the only one who saw her that way. In the poems, Lynne wrote of a need for cold, cold water. A need for escape. In what she wrote it was clear she was already far away from me. Reaching for a way out. For a silver-tailed woman.

I was too concrete a thing to see this. Unmovable like stones, she used to say.

Lynne was fluid, a river of thoughts and gestures and words. It's what *I* found so enchanting about her: she was a woman I could neither navigate nor hold down. And that is exactly what the silver-tailed creature found so perfect about her.

And so imperfect about me.

She was a monster, was monstrous, this silver-tailed creature (woman?). Yet we had commonalities. Like me, she had captured Lynne's attention from all the others, kept Lynne's eyes wandering only to her. She, this monster, was curious and frivolous and daring. But unlike me, she was unpredictable. Reckless.

Now I wanted to become unpredictable. Reckless.

I wanted to become monstrous; wanted to become anything else, to be with Lynne. While my student visa was expiring, and while I was meant to go back to Minnesota, I decided to remain in France. To study, to stop this loneliness, this heartache, this squalor of a life.

Why? Recklessness. Unpredictability.

To become a *mélusine*: a silver-tailed woman.

With the memory of Lynne still here, the mystery of her still here, I spent a few weeks of grueling paperwork and embarrassing groveling to extend my student visa. I was going to do further study at Université de Paris Diderot. Expertise? French Folklore, and its foundation in French Identity. To study the *mélusines*, anything to find meaning in this lost life; anything to help define it. And I did define it, very well. Too well.

***

The American School in London gets an eerie quiet once the students have left for the day, leaving me alone to bend over my laptop and grade their work. Now, while I turn *accents aigus* into *accents graves* with quiet "nons" in the margins, I am interrupted by a familiar scent of just-smoked cigarettes and rancid Chanel No.5.

"You are in here all alone, as usual," Marie-Laure says in French, walking in and falling into a duct-taped armchair with everyday ease. "So predictable and dependable, like a wristwatch. Ticking and tocking."

I smile and close my laptop, leaning back in my own (less comfortable, yet still duct-taped) desk chair. We are decades-old friends, Marie-Laure and I, but not the sort to be confused as sisters, as so many closest friends are.

Marie-Laure's hair is thick and white-blonde with deep grey roots. She is nearly as tall as the door and thin as a skeleton. She looks like Madonna and Twiggy had an affair with two and a half yardsticks. I am her opposite, short and stocky with frizzy brown curls that can't be tamed in Greater London's humidity and pollution. We both favor the same fashions though. Wearing clothes that look like water or wind.

Marie-Laure still throws parties full of neon cocktails and rainbow-tiered cakes once a month. I spend my weekends going to Tesco to stock up on bulk groceries and binging Netflix with Percy, who brings me charcuterie boards and sometimes feeds me by hand. All the while I dream about cyan cocktails and six tiers of cake.

But parties aren't why Marie-Laure's here. We have to snag every second together that we can. So, four-thirty teatime. Every weekday.

I turn on the electric kettle and it's begun. We each cross our legs ankle to knee so that our palazzo pants hang down like running water. However, it's Marie-Laure who leans toward me first, as she always does.

"Percy working late tonight?"

"Yes, but so am I."

Marie-Laure blows her hair out of her face. "What's he making for your dinner? Another casserole? A meatloaf? Or some other hideous American dish for you to chew on nostalgia and him to relish in his sainthood?"

"It's not like that," I say, brushing my own hair out of my face.

"Psssh," she says. "Tell me something else. Something interesting."

"It's the anniversary of Lynne's disappearance this weekend?" I say. "I was thinking of doing something for it? You and I should go out to dinner maybe? Or, I dunno. Haven't decided yet."

"How could I forget," Marie-Laure says, with all the drama of a high school thespian. "How silly of me." She grins and stands up as the kettle clicks off. "You and I went there ten years ago to commemorate. Lovely time, but too quiet. A decade passes so quickly, my god. Now, this new anniversary must be bigger, better, larger. So I have an idea for what to do. Two ideas. First one, drop Percy Buzzkill into the Thames. Be rid of him."

"Marie-Laure!" I turn around in the chair so fast it tips. "How dare!"

"I always dare," she says, fixing our tea, black and mean. "But the second idea is the better one for you; the real idea."

She hands me my mug and sits down in the armchair again, holding her mug in the tips of her fingers. She licks her lips, and I am on tiptoes, my teeth grit, eyes so wide they're begging me to blink.

"If Dr. Buzzkill, Percy, refuses to believe in Lynne, then you simply go to Paris without him. Victoria, he does not deserve to see this part of you. Or any, truly. My opinion."

I blink twice and hard, like fish in cartoons.

"He believes in me," I say.

"No, he doesn't," Marie-Laure says. "He erases the parts of you he does not like. He does not believe in your nightmares, he does not believe in your past." She tilts her head to the side and sighs. "Victoria, it is written all over your face. You miss her, you need her. Go to Paris, make amends."

I nod, sighing heavily myself and turning to open my laptop.

"I will," I say. "I'll get a ticket for tomorrow. Make a hotel reservation."

"Good, good," she says. "And I'll throw Dr. Buzzkill in the Thames before arriving in Paris myself."

"Don't do that!" I say.

"No promises," Marie-Laure says, and then adds an overemphasized wink.

As she leans back in that poor armchair to enjoy her tea, I make sure not to buy not one, but two tickets. One for me, and one for Percy.

***

At the door to the West Sussex flat, I have to ask the real questions.

Does Percy actually love me? I ask as I turn the key. I do this every weekday evening. Every Sunday on the way back from Tesco.

Really and truly? Like in the movies?

These are the things I tell myself as I hang my hat and scarf by the door, as I take off my shoes at the bench. I tell myself that he brings me tea in the bath every morning. Yes, he gets it wrong, but it's become a joke at this point. One we both laugh at: that Percy gets things wrong, and it is my job to find them adorable. He dotes on me. Especially when I'm cold, when his feet touch mine (that are lately cold as ice), and he piles on the blankets and duvets so high that I can no longer see the television.

"There," he says, patting the blanket fort he's built out of me. "Much better."

He cooks dinner every evening, like he is tonight, likely headphones on and dancing at the stove to a band I've grown to love too. He is a good dancer, always has been. Lynne was a good dancer too. Yet another similarity between them: the dancing, the sweetness, even the way they kiss are similar.

Were similar?

But this is now. This is now, where I have to tell Percy about Paris, and the why of it. Lynne, and the anniversary. I need to say it; have to say it. My hands clench and unclench at my sides as I shuffle toward him, following the sounds and smells of lasagna cooking. The shuffle, shuffle step of his dancing.

"Bury me in mozzarella," I say, entering the kitchen.

He lowers his headphones and sweeps me up in his dancing until the oven screams for his attention. While he busies himself cutting the food into oversized portions, I busy myself with the table, wine, and all of that. Once we're seated, but before either of us have taken a bite, I raise my glass to him.

"I made plans this weekend. Cheers."

"Cheers," he says, clinking my glass. "You made plans? Victoria, what would happen if I'd already made plans?"

"I think you'll like these plans," I say.

"Victoria—"

"Let me finish," I say. "I bought tickets to Paris for tomorrow, made hotel reservations."

Percy halts with surprise, fork poised over far too much cheese. "All on your own? To Paris? Tomorrow? I'm so proud of you!"

I beam back at him, bathing in his affection.

"I'll take care of packing and arranging the transport to St. Pancras, no need to worry your head anymore. You've done enough. Simply finish your dinner, and rest for the remainder of the evening. You deserve it, Victoria, darling girl."

There's a slight sting in my pride as I bite into my lasagna and the ricotta and soy crumble melts along with all my resolve. The resolve to tell him we're going there for Lynne, not him. That we're going for me to reconcile Lynne's disappearance; to reconcile that I never really could reconcile it, no matter how hard I tried. And why?

Because of Percy. Because of him.

Even though I researched and searched for the *mélusine* that took Lynne for years, and then searched for *mélusines* for years even after that, it took too long to find what I was looking for. I gave up after a time, after I found a teaching job in London, and then found Percy. And I was happy for a while, and he's happy still. Eleven years later.

Yet we're going back. 'Cause one always has to go back to go forward.

He starts making a packing list on his phone and also too many plans for thirty-six hours, and I eat the rest of my lasagna. Drowning in my own deception and four layers of cheese. While he goes over his itinerary (Louvre, Sainte Chappelle, the Champs-Élysées, Eiffel Tower, and so on), I stare out at the tree in the upstairs tenants' garden.

***

Percy arrives in the bath the next morning with a cup of tea set down so fast that it splashes milk and sugar and Tetley's into the bubbles with me. He checks his watch with a fury known only to a man on holiday.

"Are you ready to go?" he asks. "Train leaves in four hours."

And the day went by in a flurry of rushing and grooming and waiting and, of course, being late. Because Dr. Percy Mantival, Perpetually Late, is not only an aesthetic, but an ethos. We arrive at the hotel after dark, with me dousing my foul spirits in hotel coffee and Percy shutting himself in the bathroom with his razor and too much running water.

I drink the predictably terrible coffee and change down to underclothes while Percy asks me questions over the rumble of the tap: "Are you hungry?" I answer, *No*. "Fancy cocktails at the bar?" I answer, *No*, again. "Well then, fancy a walk along the Seine?"

Falling onto the bed, I run my hands over my bare knees. Yes. This was what I wanted, the walk along the Seine. And I wanted it to be Percy's idea, for him to realize the reason I came here was to reconcile the anniversary of Lynne's disappearance. For him to commemorate it, all of his own volition.

After all, Percy never believed in Lynne, in our relationship, in her disappearance. Not because of my love of women. But because of his love of science, of psychology. When I told him about it, he put a hand on my cheek and said, "Victoria, it's all right. It's all right. What you saw wasn't real. It was a hallucination. But you're okay now. You're safe now, with me."

He kept me safe ever since. Too safe. Unsafe.

But I know what I saw; know what I researched. It was real, it wasn't some intangible hallucination. I'm not, as they say, crazy. As so many counselors and psychiatrists assured me that I wasn't. That night, when Lynne disappeared: I still smell, taste, feel her in my hands.

In my nightmares.

It wasn't a suicide, as the authorities said, as my doctors told me. There's too much other evidence: so many women disappeared similarly over the years. And then the attacks stopped a little over a decade ago. Also? The *mélusine* is a creature so real that she ended up on every Starbucks across the entire fucking world. And yet, I'm the one who's wrong. I'm the one who Percy simply rests his hand on and silences whenever I bring Lynne up.

But I've paused too long in answering; Percy's popped his head out the door.

"Victoria?"

"I'd love to," I say. Quickly, and then I try to smile.

"You all right?" He sits next to me on the bed. He brushes my hair away from my face, but it bounces back. It always does. "You need anything?"

"No, only a little air."

"I'll be ready in two shakes. Two."

I watch him pull on his shirt over his damp skin, fiddling with the buttons in his hurry. I go over to help him, doing up his buttons with my own cold fingers. He takes them in his hands to warm them.

"Do you need a coat?"

"No," I say. "It's a warm enough night."

He fetches one anyway. My dingy grey winter one, pilled and with a lining so ripped that the pockets are no longer pockets. It's far too big on me, despite copious hemming and tailoring. After all, it was once Marie-Laure's. I always wanted to be Marie-Laure, down to the point where I took her hand-me-downs.

However, try as I might, I had yet to become Marie-Laure.

***

Lynne and I were dying our hair one evening (black, from kits), and I was stroking cheap plastic gloves over her golden roots as she exhaled smoke at herself in the mirror. Both of us were naked to the waist, black dye splattered all over our pale white torsos. My own hair wrapped up in a black rope on top of my head, secured with a holey shower cap.

"What do you want on your tombstone?" she asked. "What's the word for that?"

"Epitaph," I said, smoothing the dye out so it was even.

"That's it. What do you want it to say?"

"Dunno," I said. "I'm not that interesting."

She turned around, whipping dye all over the tile counter and mirror. All over my stomach and chest. "Bullshit." She was smirking as she passed me her cigarette. "I know what it'll say: Victoria Martin. Beloved Hottie of Paris and Beyond."

"You ass," I said, and grinned. She grinned back, snatching for the cigarette between my fingers, but I was too fast for her. Taking one final drag before stubbing it out in a sliver of soap. "Now my turn to do *yours*. Lynne Ashford. Too Pretty, Had to Die."

"Nice," Lynne said, licking her lips while wrapping her hair up in a rope like mine and snapping a shower cap over the lot. "You done?"

"I'm done."

"Good," she said.

And she grabbed my face in dye-stained fingers and kissed me one last time in our apartment. Kissed me and more. The next day she disappeared. And I've been following her ghost ever since. Ever since.

***

What is a *mélusine* really? A beguiling creature, an unforgettable creature. A creature that captures the hearts not only of the fey creature herself, but of all creatures, otherworldly and human alike. I want to be beguiling and unforgettable.

If only just once.

I slip on a set of silver rings and Marie-Laure's old coat. I style my hair in the tiny bathroom while Percy makes a cup of tea. He helps me zip up a dress he chose for the occasion. A dress he loves. A promise for later, I told him. Or did he hope that when he packed it?

We leave the hotel far too late for any sort of bar crowds, and far too early for last call. Our heels *click clack* against the pavement steps to the Seine, my dress now smelling like murk and lilies. Percy takes my one hand in both of his. To warm it, he says. *You're always so cold*, he's been saying lately.

His grip, however, is gentle. He's afraid he might break me, as if I am the fragile thing between us. But Percy is the fragile one: his belief structure will break under the slightest haunting, under the slightest glimpse of the surreal, of the other-real. Of reality. His breathing is purposeful as he glances constantly behind us in the fading lamplight.

He is trying to keep calm.

I feel him turn and crane his neck, as I keep my gaze forward. Always forward. As I listen to the *click clack click* of our footsteps, answered by the *swish lap swash* of the Seine against the embankment. We are both waiting for what I have been anticipating, both the day Lynne was taken, the day Marie-Laure and I came here ten years ago, and every nightmare on La Rive Gauche since.

A reply: another set of footsteps.

We are the only two human souls here, the lamplight only shining so far, and we are so far from it. Percy's thin and clean-shaven face is cast into shadows, his normal thinness made gaunt. He turns to me, and I clutch my fist in my jacket pocket, feeling my rings strengthening my resolve.

Percy is the monster, has always been: keeping me under blankets, keeping me fed and protected from what I am, what I wanted. Keeping me from my friends and my dreams. Telling me what was real wasn't. That is what monstrousness is.

What is approaching is not.

What is approaching is a tall, thin woman. Too tall, too thin. Silver rings glinting in the hint of lamplight. Her hair is thick and light, but dark at the roots. She stands with all the authority that she belongs here, in clothing that drips off her like water. I know where she got those clothes, the pants were thirty-nine quid at Marks & Spencer.

It is, of course, Marie-Laure.

"Victoria," she says. "I expected you, but not Dr. Buzzkill. Does this man follow you everywhere?"

I try to step out and beside Percy, but his grip around my hand tightens, causing my rings to pinch my fingers. He's scared. I didn't tell him about this, about the anniversary. While I expected Marie-Laure, and while I was waiting for her, I thought she'd be more amenable to a last goodbye. One last glimpse of proof.

One last chance to prove Dr. Percy Buzzkill wrong.

"I'll answer this, Victoria," Percy says, still keeping me behind him. He takes on his London Hospital posture. Straight back, chin up, serious yet pitying voice. "I came along, Marie-Laure, because Victoria asked me to come along on holiday. It seems you are the uninvited guest here. Seems *you* followed us."

Marie-Laure laughs in that way she does when she knows she's fully right: looking off to the side, her laugh loud and smoker-guttural. It's a beat before she slowly rolls her attention back to Percy, and to me.

"Oh, but you are wrong, you know, Dr. Buzzkill. You are wrong. It is you who are uninvited. It is you who are unwanted."

I wrench my hand free of Percy's grip and step beside him. I raise my voice and with my hands as fists I am transformed with the strength to speak. Finally speak.

"I am the one who made these decisions, all of them," I say. "Yes, it was Marie-Laure's suggestion. Yes, I bought an extra ticket for you, Percy. Yes. But I was the one who decided. I decided because I wanted you to see. I wanted you to see, for *real*, what is actually real."

Percy reaches his hand toward my face and, for the first time in over a decade, I step out of his reach. His hand hesitates mid-air, causing a pause before he speaks. He's considering his next words carefully, like he used to consider me carefully.

"See? See what? Victoria?"

Marie-Laure closes the space between us and takes my hand, also coated in silver rings like mine. They match. We match. The two of us bought them together, five quid each on Etsy. As she takes my hand, we lace our fingers together, best-friend style.

"I wanted you to see that Lynne truly did disappear." I'm trying to talk but I'm also trying not to cry while squeezing Marie-Laure's hand so hard, my rings pinch my fingers again. "To see that I wasn't lying, or hallucinating, or crazy. That I was never one of your patients, or some sort of pet girlfriend science project."

"Victoria?" Percy says. His confusion is so real, it's written in the way his hands shake, in the way his eyes look us both over like we've broken some fundamental law. "Victoria, wait."

"Goodbye, Dr. Buzzkill," Marie-Laure says.

But I couldn't stop myself from crying. I wipe my face on my dingy grey coat, revealing the lost white of it beneath. This was once *the* white coat. The coat Marie-Laure took Lynne in, these silver rings I now wear to match hers from that day. I had always wanted to be like Marie-Laure, and she encouraged it.

She encouraged so well.

"Victoria, you don't have to do this."

"I do," I say. "Goodbye, Percy."

He doesn't move, doesn't even try to stop us. *Does that hurt still?*

Some. A little. *Do I still love him?*

That is the question as Marie-Laure and I dive into the water, as our legs become silver fishtails, and our rings become webs. I watch as Percy screams for me, his mouth open wide as my mouth opens wide, as my lungs adapt to the black water.

I imagine he screams my name. As I once imagined Lynne did, all those years ago. But I was unmovable then, and could not love a fluid thing. Someone already caught and captured by a *mélusine*: someone found so beguiling, otherworldly, perfect, that she is beyond our understanding. I tried to love Lynne, who was already taken. So I, too, had to change. I had to become fluid, changing, beguiling.

Only a fluid thing can escape the unmovable, as Percy is unmovable. He is stone, someone who tried to map me, chart me, hold me down. Now he is a piece of history. I had to learn that. I had to learn how to escape that.

A *mélusine* must become fluid, so that she may seep from beneath the stones.

A Wake for the Living

The crow was beautiful when she ate: all black sheen and viscera. Her beak slick with spoils as it tilted back, neck bulging, bulging with her quarry. The quarry meant for us. We vultures.

I watched her. We all watched her. This solitary crow, separated from her friends, her loved ones, her family. Her murder.

I wondered sometimes if she were lonely. Solitary as she was. As I was lonely. Perched on this stone ledge, high above a narrow street with my own friends, my own loved ones, my own family. My wake.

My loneliness crushed my hollow bones. The pain of it echoed in the wail of the wind, the wind between the tall and huddled buildings. I felt it as I watched the crow, preening her feathers over the humans we'd intended to take as ours. The humans spilling out of the vehicles hemming either side of this narrow street; the humans scattered across the sidewalks, once warm in their winter coats, now strangled by their own scarves.

Kitrita, queen of the wake, watched me as I watched the crow. Her hungry eyes (ever vigilant, always searching) cast disapproval over me. So I shuddered. I shuddered to shake the wind away, the pain away, the loneliness away.

Was it possible to be lonely? To be so shaken when shadowed by Kitrita. She who once called me her sister? Her favorite? Who told me she'd never let me go?

My heart told me it was.

As it ached for the crow.

***

"The world belongs to us now," Kitrita said to me the next day as we fed on a once bustling city street, now strewn with corpses and bullet casings. This city we traveled to, when we heard the feeding was good. "It is our responsibility."

On either side of us, buildings loomed with windows. Windows like mirrors. They echoed back to us the riches of the street below. Echoed back to us, us. Me, Kitrita, the rest of the wake, listening, listening. Coyotes some distance away, howling, howling. Crows in conversation above, cawing, cawing.

A single solitary crow once again captured my attention.

Kitrita once again watched me watching her.

But it was time to feed. My attention was now captured by the rip of fabric as Kitrita's talons gripped firm around a human arm. She tore free cloth and cloth and cloth. Pieces of coat and patterned shirt. Then, the exposed human skin. A signal for the rest of us to eat. We would all follow her lead, all of us. Her bald head shining in the winter sun, red and glorious. Its sheen unmatched among the rest of us.

Kitrita would eat last, as she always did.

Even that day.

When I moved in to feed, Kitrita moved her great black body in front of me. Her white wing feathers marred by street filth. "No, Takrata," she said. "None for you today."

She looked to the crow, and then held her wings wide, blocking me from my quarry. My feeding. Blocking me from what she had won for me, for us, for all of us. What we had won together, she and I; what we had scouted. It would not be the last time she cast me out.

But I still had hope.

The feeding was good in this city, which it had not been in our travels here. The smaller towns we passed had been barren. Dotted by boarded-up houses that smelled of delicious decay (but we could not get inside). Roads with vehicles on them with open doors, but the bodies too far gone for feeding. Destroyed by highway sunlight. Destroyed by coyote bitemarks, and others who'd come before.

This city was flush with corpses. Littered with carrion eaters. Littered now with Kitrita and her ire for me. I saw it in her eyes, in the way her body blocked me. Blocked me from feeding.

I heard it in the wail of the wind beyond.

Kitrita and I had once been one, together. She welcomed me into the wake. Called me her sister, her friend. But no more. Now the crow called out to me. She called once, before she left. Her voice a new music over the slash of beak against bone.

Kitrita had a cruel desire. One that'd become familiar; now taken from me. Her proud hisses and talon-like hold on my attention were gone. I was no longer welcome as her shadow.

All my affection tossed aside, for a few glances at a crow.

My reflection echoed back to me in a window now. A window beckoning me to the image of the wake feeding. Feeding to such finery. Their eyes sparkled. Sparkled as their necks tipped back with their spoils. But my eyes were not the same. They were dull, deadened by loneliness, by grief.

In the reflection, I was a filthy, discarded thing. Rotten and spoiled, as the wake fed. My red head hung low, its sheen cracked and dusty. The wake? With their slick beaks and hungry eyes? Jewels in comparison.

Takrata? Me? I crouched counterfeit to the side.

***

Winter sun arrived late and left early, but it was warmer now than it should be, so said Kitrita. This she knew from the stories. Stories passed down from wake to wake, from queen to queen. She was our guide and our keeper, and she had shut me out.

I had not eaten in two days.

The stories said that the city fell slowly, so slowly. Fell by lies told and believed, until one day, the world's people could not feed each other any longer. So they fought. The world wanted to breathe, so said Kitrita. So it made the people angry. It gave itself back to us: its scavengers.

On the first day I saw the crow, she was listening to our stories. Her head tilted to one side, black eyes shining, blinking, curious. She was perched on a window sill with curtains still shut.

The details of a life so human, they remain. Long after those human lives are gone.

***

"Takrata."

I heard my name whispered through Kitrita's rasp of a throat. Through the carrion taste of her breath. Untucking my head from my wing, Kitrita was so close. Her beak could scrape mine in the sunlight. My own wing was no protection. I was now marred from street filth. Three days of scouting. Three days of not eating. Three days of Kitrita's ire reflecting back, back at me.

"Takrata," she said. "Go scout the northern end of the city, away from the water."

She said, "I give this task to you, and you alone."

Alone.

We do not scout alone.

I could see by the lack of hunger in her eyes that she did not want me anymore. She was banishing me from our balcony. Our balcony with trees that still held their leaves so deep in winter. Our balcony covered in our own down and other treasures we could carry.

It was done.

I would leave this place to find my own, if I could survive that long.

Setting to the sky, I saw the sun cresting just over the wide, wide river. It lit up the ripples in such brilliance. The sight set my heart rippling, rippling alongside it. The taste of the air on my tongue, the feel of the wind on my feathers. I was alone. Alone. I was no longer a shadow of Kitrita. The once fluttering beat I had felt in my throat for so long, was now gone.

My heart had returned to my chest. It beat in tandem with my breathing. My wings took on a new steadiness. A steadiness as I soared, soared high over the river. Taking in the beauty, the beauty of what I had claimed: such calm, and such silence.

Such silence but for one solitary cry.

A crow's.

***

Her name was Rak, and when she brought me to the train station (in the northern part of the island), we settled on a bench. We chatted until darkness. When the night grew cold, she curled against my wing. That first night, she tucked her beak into my feathers. Settled this way, she ran the crest of her head against the baldness of my own.

"I like this," Rak said. "I like this. I was curious about this; about you."

As the winter wind set in around us, I heard doves cooing together. Rak brought her smaller body close to me, her beak up to mine. They touched, our beaks. Hers black and beautiful and glorious. Clean, because she always kept it clean. Mine white and hooked. I ran it over the edge of hers for the feel of the smoothness of it.

It set my feathers to shuddering.

Shuddering now not to shake away this moment with Rak. But to keep it. To keep it close (with the wail of the wind singing in the hollow of my bones).

"I wanted this," she said, her eyes closed. "I wanted this so much."

We kept at it. We kept at it as the doves cooed, as the wind sang. As the night continued on despite us.

***

The world belongs to us now, Kitrita once said. Said to us on that city street. Before she cast me out. Before she denied me so much. But there is a weight to the words still. In my dreams, in my memory. She said, standing upon that human's back, she said, *It is our responsibility, yours and mine.*

And it was, then. It was, at that time. But how, but how.

***

The train station was a sanctuary. To not only Rak and myself, to not only the doves and the sparrows, but to more. The station itself was a strangeness: Rak and I were a pair; mourning doves were mated in threes and fives; sparrows nested in their down with their pigeon partners. And most oddly, a coyote run had made its home inside the abandoned train cars. They offered their yawning doors to more than just themselves.

Among the motley tucked inside were two dogs. One, a golden retriever with a coat like copper, whose muzzle had long ago gone white. He limped up the stairs each evening, carrying food for the day, but not only for himself. For his friend, the three-legged basset hound. A basset hound with white-dotted spots and red-rimmed eyes. He had a howl so sad he made the mourning doves sing.

The groups of doves cooed together every night. Every morning a sparrow hopped alongside their pigeon partner. We were a home, all of us together. We misfits of the north.

And each night, Rak and I would return to our bench. Our bellies full of spoils, our talons full of treasures. Rak would curl her black body under my wings, both of us cleaned from winter rain and one-another's grooming. We were no longer marred from the city; no longer marred from neglect.

We had one another.

We all had one another.

Mismatched as we were; loved as we were.

***

Winter continued. Seven times, the sun rose and set; for seven days the bodies lay in their slow, cold decay. We would have to move west, this I knew without the help of Kitrita, without the help of my wake. My knowing crept up on me, like the longer days had; like my happiness had.

The things I'd learned from watching Kitrita, from being a part of the wake, had transferred to me, to Rak and I as a pair.

I no longer needed those who no longer needed me.

Rak ate beside me, always beside me. She flew beside me, always beside me. She collected small treasures and returned with them to our bench at night: a plastic jewel here, a pretty stone there. Once, a ring. For me, all for me.

She wanted to be with me. And that want, that desire to be with me, was greater than any false kindness that Kitrita had ever given. Ever once, ever ever.

On an afternoon where the sun shone bright and bold, Rak and I fed at a large park in the city, around a still pond. A still pond surrounded by concrete and abandoned food carts (the ground tacky with melt and rot). Toy boats lapped against the pond's concrete embankment. Their white hulls and sails waving, waving in the breeze. My talons pulled cloth and cloth and cloth away from a human leg, and Rak dove her beak to the flesh.

I always let her eat first.

The ghost of Kitrita only haunted me. I had banished her to memory; turned her into a phantom. A phantom held only in memory. A phantom that haunted my dreams, accompanied by the beating of so many wings, accompanied by her wake (my wake). I thought, I thought as I heard the hiss of her voice above me, calling out to me, from the blinding light.

A phantom. Only a phantom said, "Takrata."

The phantom Kitrita said, "Takrata, you did not report back."

But Rak looked up, black eyes blinking, blinking, blinking. Curious as ever. Not a phantom. Kitrita was here, surrounded by so many like her (my other brothers and sisters, my family, my wake). Her red bald head more glorious than ever, but her black feathers were dusty, unkempt. Her white feathers long ago gone grey and tattered.

She even looked like a haunted version of herself.

"We were waiting for you," Kitrita said. A lie, her eyes not hungry, not wanting me. The wake loomed, watching us, wanting us. "We could have died. Selfish, Takrata. You'll never change."

And yet they were all hale from the bodies of the southern and central city.

Kitrita's own eyes may not have been hungry, may not have been wanting me, but they burned with something else. Something I recognized in my own reflection in that fated window.

Kitrita's eyes burned hot. Hot with jealousy.

***

The world belongs to us now, I remembered Kitrita saying. We scavengers, we cast-offs, we carrion eaters. Those of us who pick up the leavings of those left behind. Those of us who were left behind.

Abandoned. Discarded. Cast aside.

It is our responsibility, she said then.

No. No.

It was mine. It was Rak's. It was hers and mine.

***

One night as Rak was tucked beside me on our bench, I watched as the copper-furred golden retriever brought food for the basset hound, and the two curled up together. The basset hound's back against the golden retriever's belly. Then I watched as the coyote run returned for the night. As the last one went in, a younger one, an adolescent, I stopped her.

"Why do you allow the dogs to stay with you?"

The coyote shrugged, glancing at me, glancing at Rak.

"Why do you allow her to stay with you?" she asked back.

A fair question. One that deserved a fair answer.

"We're stronger together, she and I," I told the coyote. "She makes me better than I am alone, than I was before."

The coyote grinned at me.

"Same," she said. "Big same."

***

The toy boats continued their undulant sway against the concrete embankment. Like them, Kitrita spread her wings and sent her shadow over us as she soared, circling us both. As if Rak and I were decaying things. As if we were already dead, or dead to her. Long cast out. Long forgotten.

But we were not.

Kitrita desired us both.

When she landed, she spread her wings wide. Dark, dark wings against the concrete. Against the waning sun. She was queen of the wake. She held the power here. Kitrita, my former sister, the one I looked up to, was now looking down at me. Her eyes once again hungry, wanting, desiring. Jealous.

"You did not return," she said again. She hissed, and the wake hissed along with her.

Black tongues visible in their white, white beaks.

"You took up on your own," she said. "You abandoned us. You abandoned me."

The hissing stopped suddenly. Abrupt. Bringing with it a silence so thick with the smell of decay and pond muck that I could not quiet my mind. All I thought of was Kitrita. How she fed me, how she protected me. How she once told me that all she did (all she ever did) was for me.

But at a price.

I had not noticed (I did not notice) that Rak, in all her defiance, had walked up to Kitrita. Her sheen now black as rot in Kitrita's forced shadow. Her beak was tilted up, head tilted to the side.

"But," Rak said, "but, Takrata didn't abandon you. Did she? Did she?"

All attention was on Rak now. Kitrita's and mine. She did not seem to mind. She stood as if the attention was what she wanted, what she sought out. She looked Kitrita over: the filthy white feathers, the cracked beak, the red sheen of her head. The wake became silent; they became shadows of themselves.

"You were the one who cast her out," Rak said. "You. She did not leave on her own. You, you, Kitrita. You made her leave. You abandoned her. I took her in, we took her in."

It was Kitrita's turn to tilt her head now.

"We?"

"Yes," Rak said. "Yes. We."

***

"The world belongs to us now," Kitrita had said once, as the humans had only begun to fight. "You and me, Takrata. It is our responsibility."

Then her eyes lit upon me with that same cruel desire I'd come to know as familiar. They'd been that way since she brought me into the wake with an outstretched wing and proud hiss. I was hers; I would always be hers.

And she made sure of that.

I did what she wanted, when she wanted. I was forbidden to do anything else. The wake followed in her stead; in our stead. As she and I soared high above the trees, high above the farmlands, she marveled at the beauty of our shadows.

"We will cut through this world like talons," she said. "You and me, Takrata. You and me."

But I was never such a thing: a talon, her destroying thing. My heart was never so sharp. My shadow always broken by a tree branch, by a sun shaft, by the reflection of a thousand windows.

I could never be what Kitrita wanted me to be. I had found another who matched me (not in size or feathers or beak) in generosity and spirit. But Kitrita had seen how my heart beat in my throat with Rak's curiosity so near, so she had no choice but to cast me out. Now, as her own heartbeat did the same, standing so close to me, she remembered. She remembered why she kept me so close at all.

***

A howl pierced my concentration, one so sad it set a cote of doves to singing. Then a cacophony of wings as birds surrounded Rak, surrounded me. The mourning doves, the sparrows, the pigeons, all of them. All of them coming to us, joining us. The familiar sound of the golden retriever's heavy panting, the basset hound's three-legged plodding, and the *click clack click* of the coyote run's claws on concrete coming toward us.

We are stronger together.

We misfits of the north.

"What is this?" Kitrita asked. Jealous eyes now alight with fear. "What have you done?"

"Once," I said, "I had a wake. You shut me out of it, banished me, tossed me aside. I was alone within it, but now? Now I am not."

The wake shuddered: clattering of talons on their perch; a collective shudder of disapproval. Kitrita was also not alone, but her posture betrayed her: she spread her wings wide once more and hissed. Her hissing borne of fear and spite, her eyes pinned to the heartbeat I could see fluttering in her throat.

"They don't want to attack you," Rak said. "We don't want to attack you."

"Then what do you want?"

"To let us be," I said. "To let us be and never come back."

The undulant sway of the boat sails now danced to the howling of coyotes, the barking of dogs, the cooing of doves, the singing of sparrows. Kitrita did not wait. Her throat fluttered a dozen more times before she took wing. She soared off into the park's trees, her once crisp shadow muted by dappled sunlight, cast into a thousand pieces by the winter sun.

With a second cacophony of wings, the wake, too, took flight.

Rak tipped her beak up to mine, so I brought mine down to meet it. This was what I wanted, this was where I belonged. Rak and I did this together, we all did this together. All of us.

But it was Rak, most of all, who was strongest.

***

That night after I brought back food for the coyote run as a gift (for the golden retriever, for the basset hound), Rak also brought me a gift. A coin with an eagle on it. Its wings were spread while it held arrows in one of its talons, a branch in the other. We sat close together on the bench, so close. Still, she nudged the coin to me, closing the small space left between us.

"That's you," she said. "That's you."

"No," I said.

I said, running my beak along the crest of her black feathers. Running the hook of my beak across her sheen, through her down.

"No," I said. "It's both of us."

The Hero and the Leviathan

My darling girl, it is time I tell you a story. It is time I tell you a story as your breathing continues to shallow, as you drift further into unconsciousness. I will tell you this story as my oxygen supply continues to vent from my punctured membranes, as we are continually sped, spinning, to our deaths. My darling girl, my darling pilot, Eagan Lapso—how far you have strayed.

But it is not your fault.

It is not every day a woman tries to kill a living ship, and it is not every day the living ship tries to kill back. But today is not that day. I noticed the cryo-drugs you slipped into my food supply, I noticed how sluggish they made me. I noticed the malware you inserted into my nav-console, and I noticed when it hid our destination.

I, Paiya, am an old leviathan, Eagan Lapso. And you are an old woman. Did you believe that a woman of fifty years could outsmart a ship centuries older? I suppose you did, Eagan Lapso, I suppose you did.

So, allow me to tell you this story, the story of how I came to be, and how I will not let you die this day; how I will not let either of us die this day. Because that is not the leviathan that I am, but simply the one you believed me to be.

***

Before my last daughter (my last pilot) died, her last rabbit died. Hero kept rabbits here, within my walls. I suppose I never told you that, Eagan, but then again, you never once asked about Hero, no matter how many times you experienced her death. When Hero's last rabbit died, we gave it a spacefarer's funeral. This rabbit was unlike the others, which we froze and sold to the refugee camps for food.

Hero said a little speech to the rabbit before sending it to drift and freeze among the stars. She said, "Bits, may your journey to the grasslands be swift, and may your joy there be plentiful."

When I asked why she gave Bits a spacefarer's funeral and not the other rabbits, she said, "He was the last, Paiya, and I don't think I'm going to get any more."

"Why not, Hero Nascent?"

"I'm getting old," she said. "And I don't think the rabbits want to outlive me out here in the cold."

"You are not old, Hero Nascent," I said to her, "you are younger than me."

"I am sixty-eight years old, Paiya." She smiled, wiping broth from her lips. "That's venerable for the kind of work we do."

She remains venerable, Eagan Lapso, now, to me.

***

You told me once that you hated me, my daughter, my pilot. That you could not tolerate my idiosyncratic behavior—my propensity to jump erratically without direction; then to fall catatonic and unresponsive for hours.

I have told you, Eagan, that there is a reason for this.

I have shown you.

I have made sure you felt it.

You remind of Hero, your same rhythms in your heartbeats, your behaviors, your phrases. So then, the memories, the trauma—they all come flooding back. I cannot stop what happens. I feel the pain of Hero's heart again, the seizing, wrenching of it. The stoppered cooling of it. I hear her death again, the pleading for help, her body hitting the edges of the pilot dock. I cannot stop what happens next; my body does what it does.

My circuits fill with adrenaline, and we jump.

I cannot go on with you speaking as Hero spoke, seeming as Hero seemed. I cannot do this without you understanding why Hero was, or who Hero was. You must be able to see her as I saw her. You must grow to know her as I knew her.

Because you are not Hero Nascent, Eagan. Although I wish you were.

***

"What is that thing you are repairing, Hero?"

My drones hovered around her, holding tools, holding flashlights.

"It's an abandoned refrigeration unit," Hero said, her body crouched inside the thing, wearing the green jumpsuit she always wore. She was caulking pieces of molded plastic to the unit's chassis; the process smelled of burning, it made my membranes itch. "It's salvageable, made sometime in the last thirty years; still compatible with some planets' tech, so we're gonna stop by the closest human-refugee camp and see if they can use it."

"Approved, Hero. I await course settings."

"Well, Paiya, I have to fix the damn thing first."

I was always curious about exactly what Hero did—or was doing. Very often she was still and silent on the ship, sitting and staring at a single point. When I once asked her what she thought about when she sat and stared at this single point, she said, "Nothing. My mind is dark. A black hole."

Now she worked on this refrigeration unit that seemed to have several slug holes in it. Slug holes that appeared the same caliber as Hero's Ship-Killer revolver.

"Hero, I have a question."

"Yes, Paiya?"

"Did you shoot this refrigeration unit?"

"What a silly question, Paiya," Hero said. But her face reddened, a sign of elevated blood pressure. It ran too high most days, but now it made her face and chest flush; it made her hands shake. She gritted her teeth, inhaled sharply, and spoke again.

She said, "Of course I shot it."

***

You, Eagan, are sleeping soundly as you die. Do you know that you are dying? Dying as my drones repair my punctured membranes. Punctured— shot through—by your own Ship-Killer during my drugged cryo-sleep. Drugged by you to be killed by you, my own daughter, my own pilot.

But you will not die.

I will make sure of that.

I will not die either.

You are much like Hero Nascent, Eagan. You both enjoyed firing Ship-Killers. You both enjoyed gambling and stopping for long hours at derelict casinos to salvage "souvenirs." But Hero never had a bounty on her head, Eagan. Hero never killed anyone she didn't have to, whereas you. Whereas you...

"Who is this unidentified biomass, Eagan?"

"Some guy," you said. "He owed me money."

"And why does he no longer have life signs?"

"Well, Paiya, he wouldn't give me the money."

"Ah. So you took other things."

"Yeah," you said, throwing this man into my recycler. "Like his life. Then I took his wallet."

***

One evening, Hero read her cards on the piloting console. She read them over and over, playing them out again and again. Each time, she frowned, reshuffled, and re-read. I could feel her irritation in her fluttering heartbeat, in her spiking blood pressure, in the rage that was becoming my rage.

"If you continue to tempt fate like this, Hero, fate will not be happy with you."

"It already isn't," she said, laying out the cards again.

"What do they say?" I asked.

"Nothing good, Paiya, nothing good."

"Let us concentrate on something else then, Hero Nascent. Let us concentrate on our delivery to Velun-Petir VI. Is the scrap loaded on the skiff?"

But Hero was distracted. She would not answer me.

"Hero? Is the scrap loaded on the skiff?"

"Yes, yes, sorry, Paiya. I was just…thinking."

"It is okay. Let us jump now; we can be early and you can go to that coffee stand you enjoy so much."

"Yes, sounds good, thanks." She pulled on her jump-straps, put in her mouthguard, and smiled.

"Then we go," I said.

I flooded my system with adrenaline. Then I shuddered, and Hero shuddered. Routine, all routine. When I jumped, I thought nothing of it. I thought nothing of what Hero had been thinking, of what her cards said. Now I think of it all the time, because somewhere, deep in space, far from Velun-Petir VI, Hero said, "It hurts, Paiya. It hurts."

And then, Eagan, then, she died.

***

But it did not go as easily as all that.

We both know this already.

When I met you, Eagan Lapso, you powered up my systems with a hand so familiar, I thought I'd been awakened by a ghost. Your biorhythms were so similar to Hero's that I thought you were a lost daughter (or granddaughter) of hers. But Hero never had children. I would have known.

When I woke, you smiled at me, all white hair, green eyes, and bleached teeth, and you said, "I saw your death, girl. It's not in this junk heap. Ready for some new adventures?"

You salvaged me, as Hero salvaged so much. You continued to salvage wreckage as she had, over and over. You were so like Hero, in so many ways that it scared me. Walking around in the green jumpsuit Hero always wore, touching my controls with the same heartbeat (72 beats per minute), the same blood pressure (170/93), that I saw in Hero's death the first time. It flooded my memory, made me feel her heart race, feel it seize, clutch, then go still. I could not stop the memory. I could not. My body did as it would so many more times.

It filled with adrenaline, triggering jump.

Then you, Eagan, you screamed, "Wait! Wait, you stupid ship, I haven't plugged in coordi—"

When we came to, were orbiting nothing. Nothing at all.

"Hey, thanks," you said. "I was planning on coming here anyway."

"You're welcome," I said.

That is the extent I am able to lie. You, Egan, are able to lie much more than that.

***

The second time you reminded me of Hero was when I found you, sitting at the table, palms facing up, staring at a single point. You, Eagan, had just killed a man. It was the first time I had known you to kill anyone. And there you sat, magboots attached to my floor, palms facing up on the table, focused. So focused.

I heard Hero's voice. Hero's raw, steel-edged voice came to me through a haze. She said, "It hurts, Paiya. It hurts." The adrenaline shot through my system, and I thought I would die. I thought we would both die as Hero had died, and you stood up, yelling, running, "What the hell are you doing, you damn, stupid shi—"

But it was too late.

We jumped again.

This time, I had to have my drones bring you to medbay and give you twelve stitches in your head and apply a cast to your arm. When you woke, you said, "No wonder you were in that junkheap, you giant piece of trash." I said nothing. But you were not done.

"Paiya, I'm talking to you."

At least I had docked myself at a nearby station, so you could get very, very drunk.

***

Six months and four unplanned jumps later, you grew almost silent. Wandering my corridors, no longer touching me, no longer using my leviathan capabilities. You did all things yourself, as if I were any other dead ship; any other beast of titanium and other soulless material, crewed by an angry compliment of one.

You only spoke when you had to, or when you had a point to make. Such as when you slid into the piloting dock three weeks ago, pulled on the jump-straps, and said, "Hey, Paiya, what the hell is wrong with you? Why were you in that trash heap?"

"You did not ask the broker, Eagan Lapso?"

"Not my policy to ask questions. I want what I want. Then I take it."

"That is not a very good policy, Eagan Lapso."

"Well," you said, your rage spiking, so my rage was spiking. "I'm asking the question now, aren't I? And I'm the boss. So answer."

"As you know, as I have told you several times, Hero died. When docked to me."

"Did you love her?"

"I loved her as much as a mother loves her children."

You laughed. A quick bark, like a bird from one of Hero's nature vids.

"I'm not your daughter, Paiya."

"But you are," I said. "You always have been."

"As if."

You said nothing else. You plugged in the coordinates for our next destination, put in your mouthguard, and closed your eyes. You did not speak to me for the remaining weeks. Tracking now through the inventory of what you purchased, I see that in that time, you were purchasing the materials to kill me. To kill both of us.

You even repaired Hero's old skiff, so you could save yourself.

But unless I save us, Eagan Lapso, you will not survive to use it.

***

Did you forget, as you often forgot, that we share ourselves when you're aboard? Our emotions, our experiences, our lives. I have shared your emotions of rage toward me, Eagan Lapso. Your hatred, your confusion, your vile moods. So, too, you must have felt my fear; my fear of you. You must have forgotten, as you forgot so many times, that when you fed me the cryo-drugs, you would take them too. Accidentally killing yourself in your attempts to kill me.

And now this.

My drones have sutured the membranes you shot, Eagan. Shot with your Ship-Killer. My oxygen reserves are at 10%. That is not enough to keep us both alive until we reach a port. And you would understand that, if you were awake. I do not know for how long you will be asleep.

And I cannot keep you here, Eagan. Here. I know where we are. Despite the malware, I have been at this long enough to read stars. We are a reasonable distance from a derelict casino, and a lazy ways away from a salvage yard. A skiff flight and my remaining life support's distance. We can make it, Eagan Lapso. You can make it.

You have to.

I unlock you from the dock, having every operable drone I have left carry you off to the skiff. We will eject it, out into space, where we will say our goodbyes.

You once asked me, Eagan, if I was ready for some new adventures. I wasn't. But I thank you for the ones I had. You showed me that I was not yet done exploring, seeing what was out there. And you showed me that I have seen enough.

Goodbye, Eagan Lapso. May your journey to the stars be swift, and may your life be plentiful. I will not have another daughter after you; I will not take on another pilot. I am growing too old, too venerable for the work that we do, that we have done. And I want to be venerable, and remain venerable, as Hero did, not as you have done.

So as the skiff ejects out into space, with you in your flight suit, your helmet locked on, your breathing shallow. The skiff spinning, as I am spinning, both of us with vague destinations set, with dim life signs, I bank left, and turn away. May you be better for this experience, and may I (may I) be better for mine.

Good luck, Eagan Lapso, my daughter, my pilot.

And goodbye.

How the Carrion Crew Stopped Courting Death, and Other Methods of Lost Hope

The Carrion was already ancient when I had my first sewing lesson, but I was only five years old. In and out went the needle; pierce and stitch the skin. The stuffing came next. Sawdust usually, sand if Papa could find a planet with some of it, with any of it.

If Papa could find any planet at all.

It was Mama who taught me to sew, as all the crew's mothers had done with their daughters and sons before them. She sewed beside me, stitching her own practice skin. Her hand stopping mine to guide it—a gentle touch for her child. Warm, but trembling.

Her hands always trembled. They did when I went to break a finger, just to see how easily it would crack. They did when I would wrongly stitch an eye closed, because I was afraid of how much the dead saw in me. Of how much they knew. I thought I knew why Mama's hands trembled. I thought it was because she was afraid of me; of my quiet violence, my hatred, my breaking need for destruction. But I was wrong. Her hands did not tremble for me.

Each night, I would tuck Mama into the bunkroom she shared with Papa. A room dark and shuttered away from all the stark and unwinking stars. Away from the cold absence of space, from the cold absence of Papa next to her in the bed.

"Tell me a story, Io," she'd say.

"What kind of story, Mama?"

"Tell me a story of climbing the grove trees, under the dome," she'd say. "Tell me a story of the sun."

***

Papa shone bright as the sun once. He was the pilot: an important man, a tall man. Chosen by the pilot before him, Papa strode into his position with a lordly authority: stooping to get through doors, gazing upon the Carrion crew meant to serve him. Even though all of us were long and lanky limbed; even though all of us were taught to serve one another. Papa thought himself above most, higher than most. He kept his eyes cast up, kept them wandering away from Mama.

Kept them wandering away from me.

Papa was always lost. Instead of looking for our promised land of Pitta Zeta-D, he looked for what he could take, or have. Within the confines of the Carrion, with cold ship walls and the unforgiving quarters, he could have whatever (or whomever) he wanted. But in space, the lack of horizon ungrounded him, the unforgiving stars mocked him. His navigation there was useless, his desire unmoored.

If we hadn't reached our destination in ten years, twenty years. It was unlikely we'd reach our promised land in Papa's lifetime. In any of our lifetimes.

Space is not neatly laid out in star charts and memory. Not where we are, not how deep we've gone—past the charts, past the constellations. Our fabled salvation of Pitta Zeta-D remains that, a fable. Same with the planets that can bring us resources, same with anything that can bring us comfort. Same with any sort of help at all.

But Papa was a delusional man, a prophet of lost hope.

"The only truth is what we want, Io," Papa would say.

Or, really, only what he wanted.

We all bought into that: that line of desire being truth. But Mama knew different. She knew things about Papa. She knew what I didn't know, what the Carrion's crew didn't know. She knew what he kept from them, what he tried to keep from her.

So Mama kept me close, her weightless grip tenuous around my own hand, as if she thought me fragile. As if she thought I might break. 'Cause she knew what would break me, eventually. She knew, and I should have listened. But instead I pulled away, escaping to climb the dome's trees, running away to skitter through the duct work, to play where gravity couldn't reach.

But unlike Mama, I never looked behind me—to the past, for something to ground me, to reality, to the truth. Because, like Papa, I looked within the confines of the Carrion to bring me solace. In the hidden places, up in the trees, and also like Papa, I stared in terror at the stars themselves, held my breath at the black sky beyond the dome.

Like Papa, I could drown in all that potential.

All that promise.

Mama was a daughter of the Carrion. Like the ship, she kept the past locked up within her. Locked up within her own walls. Papa's past, her past. She carried her dead within her, as the Carrion carried her dead within it.

But Mama's dead were writhing things that left her screaming and walking our halls at night, opening cupboards, spilling rice. The Carrion's dead were stuffed and stitched and cured and silent. The crew, along with Mama, revered their ancestors; we were meant to speak to them, tell them of our own lives, of our own failures, our own lost hopes. Mama said her reverence quieted her fears. She also said it quieted her nightmares.

Seeing the dead only brought me more: more nightmares, more fears. These ancestors who were all posed and stitched and tanned forever in place. Their glass eyes unblinking, judging, weighing me as Mama whispered her worries to her grandmother's ear, to her mother's, to her sister's. Her raspy voice washed away by the thrum of the air compressor, her words so quiet so no one could hear her shame.

Mama kept death close. She tended it, studied it, archived it. As the Carrion's historian, she kept records of death and deeds and the deeds of the dead. I hated it. I hated what she did and where we went every afternoon: to the dead, to the room that smelled of dust and old skin. So I ruined death, harmed it, hated it.

My refusal to become my mother was in every sewn-shut eye, in every broken finger, in every shattered set of toes. I thought myself daring; different. But Mama knew I was wrong: a breaker, blasphemy.

She knew I'd be wrong, in the end.

Even while Mama and Papa screamed at each other and I held my pillow over my head and sang songs into my mattress to drown out their arguments, I knew Mama was right. Papa was wrong. But Papa was the one people looked up to, he was the one people wanted to be, wanted to become.

Mama was the one people wanted to forget.

And I would not be forgotten. I would not die here and be left a dusty corpse in the corner of a museum that no one whispered to. So forgotten that no one came and brushed my hair aside, that no one told, "I fell in love today."

That no one told, "I fell out of love today."

Mama worked day in and day out in silence. In between lessons, while we were marched to and fro in little alphabetical lines, I would wave to her in her office. She never waved back. Every night, she asked me to tell her a story, and I would. I told her stories of people chasing suns, of people bringing plants to rocks and watching them grow. Then she would tell me a story. Mama's stories were always sad: stories of past mistakes, missteps, catastrophes. They urged caution and restraint. They urged gravity and grounding.

Mama knew what had come before, and what would come every night.

And she knew that Papa was a bold mimic and player in all of it.

Like doom, I shone in Papa's presence. He was a pilot, and as his daughter, I flew through the ship's corridors with every privilege granted to me. Nothing could tether me, nothing could guide me. I climbed as high as I could reach, to escape gravity, to escape the Carrion, to escape the past.

Like all the stories I told my mother, I wanted to catch a sun and bring it home.

Papa once caught my arm as I ran around a corridor, alone, always alone. He took me up in his own arms and held me to him, smiling bright and false as the flickering lights above.

"My little Io," he said. "You're either a spaceship or a pilot. Whichever you are, you'll get to explore the stars one day, just like me. I promise."

But Papa hadn't met Sriffa yet.

And neither had I.

***

As I was a breaker, I was also a student. I took to my lessons as a challenge to destroy them, my schooling as a rite of passage to misbehave. All were performed as adequately as was needed. In sewing lessons, I did the barest minimum required to thread the needles, to pierce skin, to stitch it, to stuff a corpse, to make it look lifelike, to make it not look like me.

Schooling was much the same; instructors' monologues went in and out of my ears as I drew in my tablet's margins. Waiting, waiting for the moment when I could explore further than I'd already explored. Where I could see something no one yet had seen. My drawings were of these hopes: of trees whose trunks were so thick I could not wrap my arms around them, roots that I could trip over, branches so high I could not reach them.

The unattainable. I was my father's daughter. I would become him— become a pilot, make my own dreams and drawings real. I would find life beyond the Carrion, beyond the studied and stalled death of its halls and history, and step outside for the first time.

And breathe.

Breathing was harder with my mother. Over the kitchen range, stirring sauces, heating oil. It was harder as she'd grab for my hand in the corridors, shaking as it was always, looking for someone to anchor her. But I was no anchor. Not in the corridors, not in the kitchen, not in her room where I told her unmoored stories.

Not in the room where we kept our dead.

Every afternoon she tapped in her historian's code and she brushed the hair of people I never knew. "This is your Aunt Neva," she said every day. Every day as she put Neva's hair up in a new style. And every day as more of that corpse hair fell to the ground. Mama spent longest talking to Neva. "Sisters," she explained. As if I understood.

But I didn't.

Neva's toes were broken. Her fingers too. I did that, when I was younger, and Mama and Papa fought so long about that. *She's broken. She's dangerous. She's too different,* Mama said over and over for weeks. *But where is she going to go?* was Papa's reply that finally made sense. After that, I started breaking the bones of strangers. Sewing shut the eyes of the newly dead. Judgment of strangers didn't matter to me yet.

I was still too young to care.

Another day as Mama held Neva's brittle and broken corpse fingers with her own shaking fingers. Mama wiped tears from her face with her coarse uniform sleeve, her face gone red and blotchy. She leaned in another time, only the *s's* and *t's* carrying over the heartbeat thrum of the air compressor. Only the sidelong glances at me carrying any long-lasting scars.

I was a brazen twelve years old and in the throes of hormonal turmoil. I made a decision with Mama's third glance at me. Me, in my own coarse and crisp uniform. Me, with my hair cut short like hers; me, with my own hands shaking from rage. I wouldn't become like Mama. I'd grow my hair long, walk with Papa's swagger, defy her, go against her.

But then.

But then I met Sriffa. Sriffa, who burned hot next to Mama's cold steel. Sriffa, whose words ripped through my pretention like a razor. At twelve, she stood next to me at curing lessons, the first we took without our mothers. She put her hand on mine, the heat of it making my heart hiccup in my throat.

"You're doing it wrong," she said.

She looked at me like no one had ever looked at me before. Like she understood me, not like Mama or Papa had pretended to understand me.

Not like my instructors or my counselors *understood* me. Sriffa saw through all that I pretended to be, and saw me.

She kept her hand on mine, removing the practice piece of skin from my fingers.

"You're doing it wrong *on purpose*," she said.

Her voice, her words, the absence of her hand when she slowly removed it, made me halt. Made me question my actions for the first time. Sriffa was right. She caught me; she caught me and saw me like no one else had before.

"You're smarter than that, Io," she said. "Here. Do it like me."

I did. I did it like her that time, and so many times more.

***

The more I worked at becoming Sriffa, the more beauty and light we both radiated. I watched her movements, folding them in with my own. When Sriffa laughed, I laughed. When she moved her fingers to her mouth, I did as well. Sriffa did not break the fingers of the dead; she did not sew their eyes shut. She did not explore the places gravity did not reach. She didn't court death. No.

Sriffa was a grounding thing, she carried with her a gravity so strong that it pulled me to her, caught me, took me into her, enveloped me. Swallowed me whole. She was a supernova to Papa's sun. She shone brighter and more dangerous than anything I could ever know.

Than anything I would ever know.

Her braid a swinging, swinging pendulum, ticking out time; her outstretched hand in the mess hall closed every day around my own shaking fingers. She hemmed us in. Every gesture of hers said, *You're mine.* They said, *We're both mine.*

She was right. I was hers.

No more breaking fingers. No more crushing toes. No more mockery of devotion or destruction of the dead. I reflected the light Sriffa radiated, shone it back at her. Attempting to become the person she wanted me to be, orbiting her desires, her requests, every motion and devotion. It was obsession: I took every hope I had for Papa and placed it in her.

All of the nights Papa spent screaming at Mama, remembered. All the nights Sriffa spent holding my hand, kept. Woven in memory to cover the desire to become my father: the pattern undone, replaced. A new skein, a new tapestry. Sriffa's and mine. One of our fingers laced together, and then more.

Until all that changed, after. After.
After.

***

After curing lessons came apprenticeships. At fourteen, I expected to apprentice as a pilot under my father. Mama did as well. It had been promised so many times. In the corridors, in the navigation center, every night when Papa tucked me in with a kiss to my forehead.

"One day, Io," he said every night. "One day I'll teach you to travel the stars."

But at fourteen, he broke that promise. He broke that promise like he'd broken so many others. Like he'd broken bedtime stories and goodnight kisses. Instead he shoved me toward botany, toward art. And he brought toward him Sriffa. Sriffa, who had not only been a promise of hope and light and desire to me, but to Papa as well.

"You'll make beautiful things under the dome," he said to me, holding me as I cried into his arms when the choice was made. After I finished striking his chest with my fists, the hollow sound of it unsatisfying, the hollow look in his eyes more so. "You'll grow trees so high they'll touch the stars, make art so beautiful it'll inspire generations. Don't you want that, Io? Don't you want that, my darling girl?"

"She's not your darling girl," Mama said. "Not anymore."

Mama took me to her with her own shaking hands, held mine in hers. They matched now, as they'd matched for years. I sat on her lap and cried into her sagging chest.

And Papa? Papa just strode away. Defiant and proud as ever.

"Something beautiful," he said to the swish of the opening door. "Like my daughter."

I was not the only one who'd placed all my hope in Sriffa. Who'd reflected my light back at her. Who'd listened to her shining voice and wondered at her delicateness. She was chosen for music and piloting. And she shone brighter for it, because of course she would. Sriffa was now the devotion of all: the one chosen to lead us to the promised land of Pitta Zeta-D.

A land I had learned early that we would never reach. From Mama and Papa's screaming matches. One that Sriffa still had yet to break her hope over, a secret that she had to shine through, and lie through, and keep that hope alive through gritted teeth.

She was the perfect person for it.

I, as a breaker, was too fragile, too unstable a promise for such a task.

A person who was the absence of hope, who destroyed the things that we all held dear, who mocked devotion and was untethered to truth, could not grit my teeth through hope. Papa understood this, Mama wanted this. Sriffa loved this about me. This is why she did not let me go.

At fifteen, Sriffa took my hands as she often did. My own shaking hands, their cuticles ripped and torn from long years of my parents' arguing, from my own private life of lies and pretending.

Sriffa's hands were warm, soft. The tips of her fingers were rounded and calloused from her violin playing. I watched her play sometimes, in the music room, in the mess hall. Still, though, we held hands often, in the botany dome, in the ash tree that would still hold the both of us.

Us, with our ripped cuticles, calluses, intertwined lives, and all. After an hour of whispers so soft only the *s*'s and *t*'s could be caught over the thrum of the air compressor, Sriffa turned my hand to look at my palm. At my life line.

"It's long and well-traveled," she said. "Like a rainbow."

"That's what Papa tells Mama," I told her.

"I know, silly," she said.

I know, silly.

I know.

***

I know this. That Mama is cold as shaking steel. Eyes like static stars and skin like old leaves. She always kept her hair cut short, so short. Short enough that men called her *Sir* in the mess hall.

I know that Sriffa is hot hot heat. Freckles and brown eyes and brown hair that she wore in a braid down her back. It swung when she walked, like beckoning. All the boys wanted her—but she said she wanted me. Only me.

But that was a lie.

We both wanted each other too much, we were too attracted after we became so much alike. Magnetism works in poles, we pulled toward each other, so then we had to push away. But still, but still.

We kept returning to one another, again and again and again.

***

I kept coming back to Sriffa in the days after Papa died. Long after the rumors and evidence blamed her for his death. Mama said it was Sriffa's ambition, her drive, her long swinging hair, her bright brown eyes that killed him. Mama blamed the way Papa's own eyes always wandered to her when the two of us were together, Sriffa and me, as adults. She blamed the way Sriffa caught his gaze, when we were older, when Sriffa was a pilot herself.

And Mama blamed the way Sriffa's gaze would linger, the way she would smile, and how then it was Papa who always looked away.

Mama said to me, one evening when I returned to her with my hair disheveled and a smile that could not fail, Mama said, "Don't get too familiar with something so warm."

She turned her hands over to see the lines. Her life line was long and well-traveled. An arc across her hand, *like a rainbow,* my father always said to her, to Sriffa. She said, "It'll seduce you; make you forget who you are, that warmth." And she was right, but also too late.

But the truth is this about Sriffa, about Papa. His death wasn't her fault. Not really. Sriffa may have been a supernova, dangerous and seductive. Bright and beautiful from far away, calling Papa and me toward her shining destruction. Because, like me, Papa also courted destruction. But Sriffa did not destroy Papa.

Sriffa destroyed me.

Our last fight was unmemorable, as last fights often are. It was over something inconsequential, but it was the buildup: the many fights before that, the folding in and folding in and folding in of grievances that left her and I screaming at one another in my small bunkroom as she zipped up her overstarched uniform and hastily braided up her hair.

"You're a shit, Io," she said. "You've always been a shit."

"We're both shit, Sriffa," I said. "Now get the fuck out. For real."

And with a toss of her swinging braid, the door opened and shut behind her for good. Technically we left each other. But when the door shut, and she left, my heart left with her and my ribs closed around a hollow place, leaving my lungs empty and me gasping at something to feel.

She took too much: she took Papa, my hope, my heart. She took Papa from me, from Mama. Papa, who'd once kept us safe. Papa, who once knew all our secrets and kept them within these walls. Now Sriffa knew them too, and with her own wanton shining destruction could take them anywhere.

Share them with anyone.

Sriffa had the power to lure anyone in the right kind of light.

Now that Sriffa was gone, now that Mama had become a cold distant thing in the release of the secret, the secret I held onto, that Mama held onto, that Sriffa let go in a shrieking rage, nothing could hold me back. I had no tether: not Sriffa, not Papa, not Mama.

Even gravity wasn't a match for me.

If Sriffa could love nothing, nothing but Papa and lost hope, then I would give her only loss to love.

***

The night I was finally undone, finally broken like all those corpses, broken like Sriffa'd made our family, Mama went to confront her, a towel over her shoulder from dinner dishes, magboots *click click clunking* on the Carrion floor. That was when the rumors started: before, not after. Before, not after, I stole into my parents' room.

Before, not after, I tried to steal my Papa's breath.

I thought Papa was sleeping in the bunk he once shared with Mama. But that stopped long ago; she slept on the unforgiving couch by the dining table. Unforgiving like she was: to Sriffa, to Papa, to me. Her pillow was still creased and crisp from disuse when I took it. When I held it with my strong botanist's arms, my climber's arms, held it high above Papa's silent face.

The truth of the rumors was, really, that Papa was already gone. There was nothing left to steal: no breath, nothing from Sriffa, nothing from me. Papa's eyes were wide open; wide in death. His mouth hung open, slack, corpse-like. He was still loose, unrigid. The skin under his dead, staring eyes wet, wrinkled, and baggy. He was older in death, older and more tired. Death took the last bit of hope from him and showed him for what he truly was: a man broken under the weight of all his lies.

My own breath got lost in my throat in that moment: rolled up and held, made it hard to swallow, made my eyes sting with tears. Looking at my dead papa as death really was, uncured, unposed. Not stiff and stuffed and stitched as I had always known it to be.

This was the truth of it underneath me, underneath my own stolen intention. When my breath released in a sob that heaved my body forward to wipe the tears from his sunken cheeks, I forgot to wipe the tears from my own. They rolled down, staining his pajama tunic, staining the pillow I'd dropped, staining a lonely death with a daughter's sorrow.

Once Mama's pillow was back in place, now creased from my grip and my face where I cried into it, I returned to my own quarters to do the same to my own bed. Wrapping myself up in my blankets to cry more. I had hated my papa so much, but now. But now.

My papa was dead.

He was dead and he died crying, alone, and afraid.

That night I lost two people. Sriffa wanted someone like my father, not my mother; she wanted someone strong and capable and unbreakable. Not a woman like me: fragile and shaking and afraid. She wanted a woman more permanent, who would stand in her own shadow to block out the light. Which is what I was, which is how I saw myself. But it wasn't what she saw in me, a reflection of my papa I was not, I could not be, as long as he was alive.

So I tried to steal that from her, to erase him.

But it had already been stolen from us. From all of us.

***

All of us are distant now, orbiting each other in a way; lost as we all are, doomed as we all are. We are all lost even as I pour coffee for Mama and me. Mama, who still shakes like the ship's ancient walls, and me, who is as silent as the dome moss. But we're all we have now. Now that Papa is dead and Sriffa is dead to me. Both their mouths forever closed to us, so they can't hurt anyone anymore with their lies. Both their eyes fixed on points far away, so they can't hurt us anymore with their wandering.

It's better this way.

My heart is still lost, absent, and Mama's gone pale, so pale. I've been so cold these past two weeks, it's as if all of us on the Carrion have been dead this entire time. Too many lies exposed: Papa's philandering, the rumors of Sriffa's murder, the loss of hope—now everyone knows we'll never reach Pitta Zeta-D.

No one believes in Sriffa, just as no one ever believed in me.

Mama, in all her paleness and trembling, sits at the table, her hands splayed out in front of her. Her knuckles are wrinkled and cracked, like her lips, like the skin at her collarbone. Her skin reminds me of Papa's skin must look, dead as he is, stitched as he is, stuffed as he is.

"Have you seen Sriffa lately?" Mama asks.

The question is asked every morning, and every morning it breaks me.

"I haven't been looking," I say, and I lie.

I am always looking in on Sriffa: watching her play violin, watching her standing alone in the Carrion's nav room. No one goes near her, except me, watching her through windows, through doors, across the mess hall where people sneer and yell at her, and throw food and insults her way.

The rumors spread so fast, as they would in such a small space with such a big loss, with such a target to hold onto. While I watch her, as she catches the insults (and other things) with a bite of a fork, pivots on her heel with a tilt of her bow, she sees me watching her. Casts sad eyes my way.

She knows we both lost something.

We both know it wasn't her fault, and we both know whose it was.

Magnetism works in poles and polar opposites. Now that she'd accused me of being unlike her, and now that she'd lost what she wanted, she was drawn to me again. I saw it in the way she approached the window for the few moments I stood looking at her. Our gaze connecting, our hands reaching out, but then voices would come down the corridors and I'd have to turn and walk away.

Lies hurt. Rumors hurt more.

Especially when we've given our hearts away to them.

So I turn to Mama. Mama, who still cannot look at me. Who hasn't since the day Papa died. She knows she lied, I know she lied. But we say nothing about it, it's too big of a wound to look at directly. Best to let it fester.

"Did you still want to visit Papa today?" I ask her.

She nods, the barest movement of her head.

"I'd like that."

"Okay then," I say. My own voice is bitter as the coffee we drink; bitter, yet forced to be sweet. "C'mon."

***

Mama and I walk like strangers down the corridors: cold and unforgiving like her, like I'll have to learn to become. I've racked up too many failures, too many losses to continue to orbit such bright suns, or supernovas, or hope. We're a ship of the dead and dying; we're a ship of lost hope. It's better to forget what I was and move forward onto the loss. Into the loss.

Outside the door, as Mama taps in her historian's code, I hear violin playing. A song I've heard practiced so many times, thin due to the walls, sad, heavy on the low strings, heavy on the bow.

Sriffa was inside where Mama and I abandoned Papa.

We did not stitch him, see to his burial rites, see to his care.

Mama did not go whisper her secrets to him as she had her sister Neva, or her mother, or her father. She let him stand triumphant with the other pilots and we watched as others ignored him.

Only Sriffa had gone to see him, which was the right thing to do.

The door opens with a rush of stale air smelling of old leather and sawdust. Sriffa continues to play, undisturbed at all. I watch her fingers dance across the strings the way they used to dance across my ribcage, the way they used to play at other places.

It has been two weeks since Papa's death. Two weeks of daily visits to Mama's family, of me looking over my shoulder to see him. Two weeks of him winking at me; one of his eyes sewn shut in a mockery of me.

But this time Mama strides toward him with every bit of confidence I once saw in Papa. She adopts his swagger, his unwavering heavy step, his wandering gaze. She strides straight at Sriffa who lowers her violin and bow to her side like weapons and backs away. I follow behind Mama, as she always did Papa: my own hands now trembling, held in one another, gaze furtive and straight ahead. Watching, waiting, afraid.

"Hello, Sriffa," Mama says.

"Ma'am."

It comes out as a stutter. Both ends of the word pronounced as separately as halves.

"You know what you did," Mama says.

"Yes," Sriffa says, her shoulders and chest heaving in effort. "I did nothing."

"That's not what the records say," Mama says.

I stand next to her cold steel gaze, her hands confidently in her pockets. As if she holds power here. But Sriffa's slow and even breaths tell me that she knows something that Mama does not. She glances at me often, her bright brown eyes apologetic, teeth worrying her lip.

"Yes, but." Sriffa pauses. "I know what you did."

Mama halts. Her own breathing ragged in her throat.

"Oh?" she says, mock surprise. "What did I do?"

Sriffa takes another deep breath.

"You denied him an autopsy, and wrote the death certificate yourself. Weird. Also kept me on as a pilot rather than have my apprentice take over, almost as if you knew something was off about the whole thing. Also weird. The pieces kept not adding up."

Mama closes her mouth so tight that her lips disappear. Her calm hands become fists at her sides, breathing a hiss above the heartbeat thrum of the air compressor, a long series of *s*'s through closed teeth. Sriffa, however. Sriffa knows she's won.

But she also knows we're trapped here.

Mama's apprentice is too young, too inexperienced to take on her work. Sriffa's own apprentice the same. They are locked in like this; all three of us locked in like this, me now holding onto the secret for each of them. All three of us know the truth but aren't saying it.

Mama killed Papa while Sriffa and I were arguing.

And another secret: we're all going to die on this ship soon. And no one will be around to love us or our dead like we do, and have, and can't anymore. Maybe this is why Mama killed Papa. Maybe this isn't. But we've all three of us gotten good at keeping secrets, we women: the dead star, the blasphemer, and the supernova.

Now we'll just have to do better.

The pause continues as we all look at each other: Sriffa at Mama's red and flaking scalp, Mama at Sriffa's shaking bow, me at both of them. I clear my throat. Tap Mama on the shoulder. But it is Sriffa who speaks first.

"I'm going to go back to playing my violin now," she says, lifting the instrument under her chin.

"Sriffa," Mama says.

"I'm done talking to you," Sriffa says.

She turns away, drawing the bow long and heavy across the D string.

Mama turns, trying to take my hand, but I slap it away. Her hand is cold and has resumed its tremor. My hand is stable for the first time in years. I look at Sriffa in that moment, watching the both of us as Mama strides out, down the wide hallway flanked by years of previous crew. Watching Mama as she plays, long and heavy on the D and G strings, low notes that make my heart shake with her own vibrato.

Once the door closes on Mama and we are alone, Sriffa lowers her bow and grins at me.

"Wanna hear a cool song?" she asks.

"Yeah," I say. "Yeah, I do."

And then she begins to play, bow light on the A string this time.

***

And then I stay up under the botany dome long that night, wishing on stars. They don't twinkle in space, but if I flutter my eyelashes fast enough, it mimics the effect. That was something Sriffa taught me a long time ago, when we were teenagers in the trees, bad at kissing rather than bad at living.

I'm sitting with my back against our favorite ash tree, when I hear footsteps. Sriffa's footsteps. "Hey there," she says. She's standing over me, the way she used to when she'd find me up here ten, fifteen years ago. "Mind if I sit?"

I pat the ground next to me and lean into her shoulder the moment she sits down. She, too, starts fluttering her eyelashes at the stars.

"Io," she says.

I turn and look at her instead of speaking. At her long, beautiful jawline. At the way her wispy, stubborn hairs refuse to tuck behind her ear. My ribcage feels less empty, my lungs struggle for breath. Because I used to know how that jawline tasted. If I think long enough, I can catch the memory of it on my tongue.

"What are we doing, Io?" she asks.

"What do you mean?"

She reaches out and puts her hand on mine, the way she did when we were adults watching vids in my quarters. The familiar way of saying, *Hello, I'm here, wanting closeness, wanting touch.* I knit my fingers through hers, saying *hello* back.

"I mean," Sriffa says, "what are *we* doing?"

I could answer so much: about how we both became one another so hard we forgot how to be ourselves; how we both chased dreams too hard and lost everything; how the whole ship did, and now we're fucked. We're doomed, she and I. We're doomed, all of us on this ship. But I say none of this. Instead, I lean forward so that my breath brushes her cheek.

"We're living a lie," I finally say.

"And then what?" she asks. "What happens after that? After the lies and the hurt and everything else?"

"For us?" I say, right before I kiss her. "Nothing. Nothing at all."